SEARCHING
FOR
Lottie

SEARCHING FOR
Lottie

Susan L. Ross

Holiday House • New York

HOLIDAY HOUSE is registered in the U.S. Patent and Trademark Office.

Printed and bound in November 2018 at Maple Press, York, PA, USA.

Photograph on page 170 courtesy of the author's private collection.

www.holidayhouse.com

First Edition

1 3 5 7 9 10 8 6 4 2

Library of Congress Cataloging-in-Publication Data

Names: Ross, Susan L., author.

Title: Searching for Lottie / by Susan L. Ross.

Description: First edition. | New York : Holiday House, [2019] | Summary:
"More than six decades after the end of World War II, twelve-year-old
Charlie, a budding musician, searches for clues about her violin-prodigy
namesake's fate"—Provided by publisher.

Identifiers: LCCN 2018030894 | ISBN 9780823441662 (hardback)

Subjects: | CYAC: Family—Fiction. | Violin—Fiction. | Musicians—Fiction. |
Jews—United States—Fiction. | Holocaust, Jewish (1939–1945)—Fiction. |
Jews—Austria—Fiction. | Austria—History—1938–1945—Fiction. |
Mystery and detective stories. | BISAC: JUVENILE FICTION / Historical /
Holocaust. | JUVENILE FICTION / Mysteries & Detective Stories. |
JUVENILE FICTION / Biographical / European.

Classification: LCC PZ7.1.R73 Se 2019 | DDC [Fic]—dc23 LC record available
at https://lccn.loc.gov/2018030894

In memory of Charlotte, her spirit ever bright

Vienna, January 1936

"Keep your voice down, you will scare the children!" Mutti's muffled words drifted through the thick plaster walls of the small apartment.

Lottie stood in her tiny bedroom, practicing the violin. She lowered the instrument, straining to hear.

"The Nazis are gaining strength. We must act now, before it's too late." Papa sounded sad and strangely old.

"We cannot leave," Mutti replied. "Think of Lottie's future! Have you forgotten what her tutor called her? 'A bright star; the finest pupil at the music academy.'"

Lottie sighed and tucked the violin back under her chin. So much talk about the Nazis and whether there would be war. What did it all mean? She began the sonata again but quickly stumbled. "Miserable fingers!" If only it wasn't so very cold; she could barely feel her hands. But times were hard, and there was never enough coal to heat more than the parlor. The Winter Competition was less than a week away, and if she wanted to keep her scholarship, her performance would have to be perfect. The bow must float on the strings; every note must sing.

The bedroom door creaked open slightly, and a small nose appeared.

"Is there a mouse at my door?" Lottie asked.

"Yes, squeak, squeak!" the voice responded. Chubby arms pushed through the doorway, revealing a tow-haired child in a nightgown. "I saw one today," Rose said, "a mouse in the kitchen."

"Don't tell Mutti." With a finger to her lips, Lottie smiled.

"May I watch you practice?"

"In a minute." Setting the violin on the narrow bed, Lottie grabbed her little sister by the waist, lifting her up into the air.

"Higher! I want to go higher!"

"Enough?" Arms reached toward the ceiling.

"More! Mice like to fly!" Rose giggled.

"Do they?" Two long twirls were followed by a bumpy landing on the carpet; the little mouse lay on the floor laughing and squeaking.

"Why is Papa so sad?" Rose asked, suddenly serious.

"What do you mean?"

"Mutti and Papa are always stern." Rose rolled up, her head propped on her knees. "Mutti won't play with me, and Papa doesn't smile anymore."

"Everything will be fine again soon, I promise." Dropping

to the floor, Lottie tickled Rose's belly and then pulled her into her lap. "Grown-ups worry far too much, that's all."

Rose nestled into the warmth of her sister's arms. "Can you rub my fingers, pretty please?" Lottie took the small, pudgy hands between her own and blew on them. She glanced at the frost accumulating on the long windowpanes; the sky was as gray as the buildings surrounding them, and tiny flakes of snow were beginning to fall.

When she was certain her sister's fingers were warm, Lottie sprang to her feet. "Now, that's quite enough talking!" She picked the violin up from the bed. "I won't win the competition by chatting idly on the carpet. You come keep the sheet music still for me, little mouse, and I'll get back to practicing."

CHAPTER ONE

Hillmont, Connecticut, September 2010

"Is this the girl who died?" Charlie asked softly. She held up a faded black-and-white photograph of a young girl wearing a flowered dress with a white lace collar. The girl had large, shining eyes and a mischievous grin.

"What was that?" Mom stopped short, her arms full of laundry.

"Is this the girl I was named after?" Charlie sat cross-legged on the couch in the family room beside the kitchen. Headphones held back her long red hair; an oversized photo album rested on her knees.

Mom set the laundry on the kitchen table. "Let me see." She glanced at the old photo and sighed. "Why are you looking at these today?"

"School report." Charlie pulled the headphones from her ears and pushed her corkscrew curls to one side. "You know how all the seventh-grade social studies classes do a family research project for the first assignment of the year? Jake did his on Dad's great-grandpa from Lithuania, remember? It turned out he was a lawyer just like Dad."

"Are you talking about me?" Jake bounded into the room, his mouth full of chips. He was endlessly tall and equally annoying. "And how I totally aced that project...?"

"Absolutely not and could you please go away?" Charlie's eyes flashed.

"Hey, what are you listening to?" Jake frowned as he strained to hear the sounds coming faintly from the headphones on the couch. "What the—Charlie, is that *classical* music? Why do you *listen* to this stuff? Is that like, an *opera* or something?"

"It's Mozart!" Hot-faced, Charlie hit the pause button on her phone to silence the music.

Jake mumbled something about musicians being temperamental and went to check the refrigerator.

Mom sat down beside Charlie. "Okay, I remember Jake's project now. Tell me more about yours, and what you're considering."

"Well, you know we have to choose a family member to research, right? So I'm thinking of picking the other Charlotte—the girl who died in the Holocaust. The one you named me after."

Charlie passed the album to Mom, who slowly turned the pages. Each one was filled with fading faces staring out from a different time. The women wore calf-length dresses, and the men were outfitted neatly in suits, with vests and pocket watches. Mom paused at the photo of a smiling teenage girl with long banana curls pulled back in a large white bow; the girl was holding a violin. "Here she is again," Mom said. "This is Lottie."

"Lottie? Not Charlotte?"

"Lottie was a nickname for Charlotte, and that's what everyone called her." Mom hesitated. "We were going to call you Lottie, but your brother said it sounded too old—it was Jake's idea to use the name Charlie."

"Oh, I didn't know that!" Charlie cocked her head as she examined the photograph. "She looks pretty."

"She was very pretty, I think," Mom replied. "She had lovely eyes like you and dimples around her mouth the same way you do. And of course, look at her hair—both of you have those gorgeous curls." Mom smoothed the bangs of her own straight brown hair and smiled.

Charlie squinted as she inspected the picture. "I don't think she looks *exactly* like me. I have red hair; hers is dark. Maybe our eyes are a little the same...hers might be blue." Charlie looked up. "Lottie was Nana's sister, right?"

"Yes, Lottie was several years older. Your nana told me how clever she was; how determined...just like you." Mom smiled. "And here's another thing you two have in common— Lottie played the violin. In fact, Lottie played so beautifully that she performed with the Vienna Philharmonic when she was a teenager."

"Seriously?" That was a weird coincidence. Violin was *her* thing, too. Charlie had begged her parents for lessons when she was still in kindergarten. She'd always loved music, and she liked pop and hip-hop as much as any kid at Hillmont Middle School . . . but there was something about classical that made her heart skip. She could lose herself in a symphony in a strange way that she never tried to explain to her friends. Only her best friend, Sarah, understood that feeling, but Sarah had moved to Boston over the summer.

"I guess she must have played *a lot* better than Charlie does." Jake stood in the arch between the kitchen and family room, gulping down a Gatorade. "Charlie stinks at the violin!"

Charlie flung a pillow, though it fell short of its mark. She might not be nearly as good as Lottie had been, but she sure didn't *stink*.

"Jake, don't you have homework to do?" Mom's voice sounded strained.

Jake rubbed the cowlick at the top of his towering head and grinned. "Finished an hour ago."

Charlie tugged on Mom's sleeve. "What else do you know about Lottie?"

"Well, the family was from Vienna, the capital of Austria. Her father was a math professor at the university."

"And . . . what *exactly* happened to them?"

Mom hesitated, then let out a long sigh. "Honestly, I'm not entirely certain. When the Germans invaded Austria, the Jews were at the mercy of the Nazis. I know that Lottie was lost, along with my grandfather. My grandmother and Nana Rose were lucky to escape. They came to America on a ship."

"So Lottie died...right?" Charlie swallowed hard.

"Yes, I guess she must have." Mom looked uncomfortable.

"You guess? You don't know for sure?" Charlie sat up straight. She searched her mother's blank face and glanced down at the photo. Lottie's eyes were bright, with long dark lashes, and they were staring up at her.

"The truth is that nobody knows exactly what happened to Lottie," Mom finally answered. "But entire families perished. Nearly all of our family members who couldn't leave Europe were killed." She began carefully folding laundry.

Charlie took a deep breath and frowned. "If she lived, Lottie would have to be very old by now."

"Don't you get it, Charlie?" Jake asked, suddenly serious. "She must have died. You couldn't possibly find her alive, and you probably wouldn't find out anything new about her, either. You'd be better off picking somebody else."

Charlie threw another pillow from the couch; this time it soared slightly shy of Jake's head.

"Sweetheart," Mom said gently. "You have to understand that even if you do learn something new, the ending of this story will be very sad. The Holocaust was a tragedy that touched every Jewish family."

"Mom, I'm twelve. I'm old enough to know."

Mom smiled a sad sort of smile—proud and worried at the

same time. "Are you *absolutely* sure you want to research Lottie? Because you could do a terrific report on—"

"I've decided, Mom. I want to find out more about Lottie—who she was and what really happened to her." Charlie crossed her arms. "I'd better get in touch with Nana Rose to get started. I'll think up some questions to ask her."

Mom nodded. "Well, we'll be visiting Nana at her new retirement community in Florida in a couple of weeks. Do you want to call in the meantime?"

Charlie shook her head. "Not for this. Nana Rose has trouble hearing me. And she always gets mixed up over the phone."

"Once, she thought I was her accountant," Jake added.

"Do you have time to write?" Mom suggested. "She loves getting letters."

Charlie nodded. "Yeah, I have a whole month—the report's due the first week in October. Hey, what's this?" Mom had flipped to the last photograph in the album, which was a picture of Lottie in the park. She looked about six or seven and was playing with an old-fashioned top dangling on a string. Charlie touched the plastic covering the photo. "I think Nana gave me a toy just like this when I was little!"

"It's called a diabolo," Mom replied. "You loved tossing it way into the air and catching it above your head, remember? You practiced and practiced all summer and wouldn't come inside, even when it got dark."

"It's funny that Lottie and I liked the same toy." Charlie paused, then slipped her headphones back on. Music filled her head once more. She could see Jake out of the corners of her eyes, conducting in the air with a fake baton and snickering.

Charlie looked the other way and turned up the volume for the last movement of the symphony. It was her favorite part— the string section swooping and swelling until her pulse raced along with the music.

Lottie must have been amazing on the violin if she had performed with the Vienna Philharmonic! Charlie got nervous just playing at her school concerts.

Charlie shut her eyes and shuddered. How could a girl like *that* simply vanish?

CHAPTER TWO

Dear Nana Rose,

I hope you're feeling well and that you like your new home at Clover Manor. We'll be coming to visit you soon, and I can't wait. I have a question. I am doing a school report about our family, and I want to learn more about your sister, Charlotte, the girl I was named after. Could you tell me a little bit about her?

Mom says she was a great violinist. What was her favorite music? What happened to her?

I hope this doesn't upset you, because I already know that it's a sad story.

Love, xoxo,

Charlie

After mailing the letter to Nana Rose, Charlie taped a sign on her bedroom door: JAKE KEEP OUT.

She set the timer on her phone to exactly one hour, took out her violin, exercise book, and sheet music, and began to practice. Auditions for the school string orchestra were in two weeks, and she had to be ready. For now, seating in orchestra class was relaxed and informal. In the half-moon of folding chairs surrounding Mr. Fernandez's podium, students could take any stand they wanted, so long as it was in their instrument section. But after auditions, Mr. Fernandez would organize the orchestra according to skill. The best violinist would become concertmaster, and the best cellist and violist would take first stand in their sections.

Charlie had practiced nearly every day all summer and knew she was one of the most advanced violinists. She'd picked a challenging audition piece—a section of Mozart's Violin Concerto No. 3 in G Major—and she thought she had a decent shot at making concertmaster. Her only real competition was Tommy Lee, an eighth grader who claimed to practice his violin two and a half hours every night after school and three hours on Sundays. Tommy's bowing skills were first-rate, and his rhythm was good, but his intonation wasn't perfect—every once in a while, he played slightly out of tune. Charlie thought if she tried hard enough, she could do better. But there were no guarantees.

After an hour, Charlie's bow arm started feeling heavy and her shoulders began to ache, but she only stopped to stretch her neck once to either side before turning the page. Sarah would be proud of her for working so hard, Charlie thought.

Sarah played the viola and went to music camp in Maine every summer. When they used to practice together, which was nearly always, Sarah would insist they keep going until neither one of them missed even one note or went off tempo.

The girls had been a musical duo ever since meeting in orchestra in fourth grade. They'd made a pact to form a chamber group someday called the Chamber Chicks. Whether or not to include chamber dudes was the source of endless discussion.

Charlie knew it was going to be lonely in orchestra this year without Sarah, but already, only a few days into seventh grade, it was even harder than she'd expected. Charlie had two other close friends, Hannah and Amy, but Hannah was into sports and Amy was president of the science club. Neither one played an instrument. They'd come to watch Charlie and Sarah's spring orchestra concert last year, but she could see them poking each other and whispering during the performance. Classical music wasn't really their thing.

When the timer went off, Charlie took a deep breath and kept practicing. Five more minutes! She played a section from *Eine kleine Nachtmusik*, the performance piece that her orchestra class was working on, four times over without any mistakes and finally stopped. Not too shabby! Tomorrow, she promised herself, she would practice even longer.

Charlie rubbed the calluses on her fingertips and thought about her family history report. She wanted to talk to Sarah about her project, too. Only Sarah would understand how badly Charlie wanted to be like Lottie—the very best on the violin.

Charlie picked up her phone and texted:

Doing research on Nana's sister, Lottie. She disappeared in the Holocaust and nobody knows what happened.

Sarah responded with a broken emoji heart. **Wish I was there to help! Keep me posted.**

Charlie smiled and stretched out on the green shag rug under her desk. Time to focus. She opened a new red binder and printed *FAMILY HISTORY PROJECT* in black marker on the front. In it, she intended to write down every detail she could remember about Nana Rose and their family.

What was Nana's mother like? Charlie chewed the top of the marker, thinking. The highlight of Jake's bar mitzvah had been an enormous Viennese table overflowing with fancy layer cakes and cookies. Nana Rose was practically world-famous for her apple strudel; did she use her mother's recipe? Charlie made a note to find out.

And what about Nana's father, the math professor? Charlie had somehow always known that he had been killed by the Nazis, but she couldn't remember who told her. Was it Jake? Mom and Dad didn't ever talk about sad things. Sometimes, Mom would even turn off the TV if a show was too violent or depressing. And Nana Rose almost never said anything that wasn't happy or cheerful.

Once, when her parents were away, Nana Rose had helped

Charlie with her math homework. The last problem was especially tricky, but when Charlie got the answer right, Nana smiled and said that a mind for figures was something you got from your genes.

Charlie sighed. Was that all she could think of? She tapped the page with the end of the marker, trying to remember more.

A tiny sliver of memory seeped into her brain. It floated in with strands of music, a Brahms concerto from a moment nearly forgotten. Every winter before Nana Rose moved to Florida, she used to take Charlie to a concert at Lincoln Center in New York City. It was their special outing, just the two of them. Nana Rose would carefully explain the program and tell Charlie all about the conductor, the wonderful musicians in the orchestra, and the pieces they would play.

One time, when Charlie was little, a young soloist came onstage to perform. Charlie remembered that she was tall and pretty, with long wavy hair that fell below her waist. The girl was breathtaking on the violin. Her body seemed to melt into the instrument while her bow moved backward and forward like a graceful extension of her arm. The concerto was difficult, but the melody rang out pure and joyful.

When the girl finished playing, the whole audience jumped to its feet and cheered. Charlie clapped and yelled *"Brava!"* but when she turned toward her grandmother, she was shocked to see that tears were rushing down her face faster than she could wipe them away.

"I am sorry!" Nana's voice was trembling. "That lovely

girl reminds me of someone very dear, that's all." Nana Rose touched her chest. "Her music comes from here, inside the soul." She traced Charlie's forehead with her fingertips. "You, too, have this gift, my darling. Someday it will be you upon the stage."

For Hanukkah that year, Nana Rose bought Charlie her first violin. On the card, she wrote: *Carry music in your heart, and love will never perish.*

CHAPTER THREE

After Charlie finished writing down every detail she could remember about Nana Rose and her family, she picked up the red binder and went into the upstairs hallway. It was time to see what Jake might know. She walked by his room twice before knocking.

"Busy! Go away!" Jake yelled.

"What'd you say?" Charlie took a deep breath, scooted through the doorway, and plunked down at the end of Jake's extra-long bed before he could protest again.

Jake's room always looked like a hurricane had just passed through. Nearly every inch of the walls was covered in basketball posters, and the floor was littered with jerseys, gym shorts, and gum wrappers. Jake was lying with his iPad on a rumpled bedspread, his long legs sprawled over the sides of the bed.

"I need to ask you something." Charlie pulled a piece of bubble gum from her pocket and held it out in the palm of her hand. Fruity mint, Jake's favorite.

Jake grunted as he popped the gum in his mouth. "Okay. I guess."

"What do you know about Nana Rose's childhood?"

"Huh?" Jake propped himself up on his elbows. "What do you mean?"

"Nana's never told me about her life when she was young. I mean, before the war. So, I was wondering..." Charlie paused. "Do you remember her saying anything?"

Jake chomped on the gum, thinking. "She liked hiking in the Alps with her dad."

"Are you sure?" Charlie was shocked. Nana Rose adored music, but she'd never once mentioned hiking.

"Yeah. Remember that time I went with the Boy Scouts to Vermont? Nana loved hearing about that. She told me her father used to take her to the mountains. It was his favorite place."

"Did she say anything else?" Charlie inched forward. "About her family—or Lottie?"

"Hmm." Jake snapped the gum under his tongue thoughtfully. "After my bar mitzvah I heard Nana Rose talking to Mom. Nana said it made her sad that Lottie couldn't be there." Jake frowned. "She said she hated to think about Lottie missing everything, like her wedding to Grandpa Sam, our getting born... all the family stuff."

"It must have been really hard for Nana to grow up without her sister and her dad." Charlie sighed.

Jake blew a large bubble and sat up straight. "Did you know that Nana Rose and her mom had a bakery? Somewhere in Brooklyn. Nana worked there until she married Grandpa Sam."

"A bakery? Seriously? Are you sure?"

"Hundred percent! Don't you remember the chocolate rugelach she made for my bar mitzvah?" Jake patted his stomach. "The rabbi ate four pieces!"

Of course, Charlie thought. That made so much sense—Nana Rose was an incredible baker, and she never, ever came to visit without bringing delicious cakes or cookies.

"So...what about Grandpa Sam?" Charlie asked. "He died right after I was born. Do you remember anything about him?"

"Only a little," Jake said. "I remember he had a bushy moustache, and he liked ice cream. One time he took me to play mini-golf...I wish I could remember more."

"He must have been nice." Charlie liked ice cream, too—a lot.

"He was married to Nana Rose," Jake replied. "He must have been awesome."

CHAPTER FOUR

Charlie was in the family room practicing scales on Thursday afternoon when the doorbell rang. She had nearly finished the D-minor scale but shifted her hand a little too far and missed the final note with a hideous twang. Not good! If she wanted to be concertmaster, she would have to do a lot better than that.

Peering through the window, Charlie could see the mail truck in front of the house. She quickly opened the door with her violin tucked under one arm.

"Hello there. Is this the residence of a professional violinist?" The mailman pointed at the violin as he held out a small package.

"Someday . . . maybe?" Charlie blushed.

"I've got something addressed to a Miss C. Roth—can you sign for it?"

Charlie signed, grabbed the box, and ran up to her room. The address was handwritten in large block letters. Inside, there were three folded pieces of stationery sitting on top of an object wrapped in tissue. She sat cross-legged on her bed and carefully opened the letter.

My Dear Schnuckelpuss,

I am delighted to hear from you! How does it feel to be in the seventh grade? It seems like yesterday that you were the most beautiful baby in the world. Such gorgeous red curls you had! Such bright blue eyes! Everything is fine here at my new home, Clover Manor. Perhaps it's a little bit quiet, that is all. I miss you, too, and I am counting the days until you come to visit.

On the topic of my sister, Charlotte—yes, it is a sad story, but it fills my heart with joy that you want to know more about her. Lottie was eight years older, so I looked up to her in every way. Children especially loved her. She was intelligent and beautiful, and played the violin like an angel. Your mother must have told you that as a teenager, Lottie was asked to play with the symphony in Vienna, the finest orchestra in Europe! I kept a book of her newspaper notices, but I am having trouble finding this. I will keep searching, and show it to you when you come to see me in Florida.

Charlie stopped and imagined Lottie playing on the stage of a grand concert hall. She smiled and made a quick note in her binder before finishing Nana's letter.

As to your question, what happened to my sister? I must tell you that yes, it is still very painful. I loved my sister dearly. And Lottie was so talented! My parents sent her to continue her music studies

in Budapest. She was to study with Herr Hinkleman, the head of a famous music academy there. Then the Nazis came to Vienna. No Jewish person was safe. My dear father was arrested, and my mother and I fled for our lives. It was a terrible, terrible time.

There were smudges on the page over the word *terrible.* Charlie's heart began to pound as she picked up the letter again.

We were not able to reach my sister. My poor mother was frantic, and I was only a little girl. We had no choice but to leave Austria as soon as we could. There was no war yet in Hungary, and we prayed that Lottie would remain safe and would someday join us in America. My mother wrote many letters to Herr Hinkleman but received no reply. After the war, Mutti contacted the Red Cross and learned that my darling father was gone, but there was never any word about Lottie.

My darling Charlie, we never found out what happened to my sister. This remains my greatest sorrow.

I am so happy now that you are thinking of her. I loved her very much and carry her with me, always.

I am sending you Lottie's most prized possession, which I brought with me when we came to America. We could each take only one suitcase, but I believed that I would see her again, and I knew that this was precious to her. You should have it now, since you are her namesake and so like my dear sister in your heart—and in your music. I will explain more when I see you, but in the meantime, please keep it safe and remember her.

Much love, xoox,

Nana Rose

Charlie carefully unwrapped the tissue. Underneath several layers of neatly folded paper lay a dark green notebook with a creased leather binding. The cover was worn and tattered at the edges; its yellowed pages were filled with swirling script. She guessed that the language was German. But what was this notebook? Could it be Lottie's *diary*? If so, what would it reveal?

"Mom, I need you!" Charlie dashed up the stairs. Mom worked part-time selling real estate, and Charlie knew she hated being disturbed in her home office—but this couldn't wait. "Nana Rose sent this to me! She says it was Lottie's. I think it's her diary!"

"A diary?" Mom pushed back from the desk and took the notebook from Charlie's outstretched hands. "Are you sure this belonged to Lottie?" Her brow narrowed into a dark line as she carefully opened the old notebook, revealing, on the very first page, a name and date: *Charlotte Kulka, 1938*. "I can't believe it. My mother never showed this to me."

"Nana says she wants me to keep it because I'm Lottie's namesake. Maybe it will tell what happened, or at least have some clues." Charlie touched the handwriting gently.

"Nineteen thirty-eight was the year that Austria was seized by the Germans. After my grandfather was deported, Nana Rose and my grandmother barely escaped with their lives," Mom said in a hushed voice. "I had no idea they were able to save anything."

"You never asked?" Charlie wondered aloud.

Mom sighed, a faraway look in her eyes. "Sometimes Mama would share a happy memory from her childhood— mostly she loved to recall Lottie's musical accomplishments.

She was extremely proud of her sister! But then it would make her so sad thinking about what happened to her family that . . . well, I knew better than to ask anything more."

"Could you read this for me?" Charlie pointed at the notebook.

"I'm afraid not. I can say a few words of greeting in German, but that's all."

"What should I do?" Charlie stared down at the swirling letters as if they might translate themselves if she concentrated hard enough. "Nana says she'll tell me about it when we see her, but I don't want to wait that long."

"Well, maybe you could try an online translator, but with this old script, I doubt it would work. What about a teacher at school?" Mom suggested.

"We only have Mandarin and Spanish." Charlie bit her bottom lip, thinking hard. "I know—I can ask Sophie!"

"Sophie?" Mom looked confused.

"Yeah, you know how Hannah's family has an au pair who watches the baby? Her name is Sophie, and she's from Switzerland. I think she speaks German. I'm going to text Hannah right now!"

"Good luck," Mom called out, but Charlie was already down the stairs and on her phone.

After Charlie texted Hannah, she sent a quick message to Sarah, sharing the news. **Keep your fingers crossed!**

Double crossed! Sarah immediately replied.

CHAPTER FIVE

Hannah called Charlie practically the minute she got Charlie's text. Charlie told her all about Lottie and how Nana Rose had sent her Lottie's old notebook, which she hoped was a diary.

"I didn't know you were named after somebody who died!" Hannah exclaimed. "Charlie, that's terrible."

Might have died, Charlie whispered in her head. "Yeah, it's kind of hard to believe sometimes." Charlie sank down on the couch. "The strange thing is that I never knew Lottie—or even thought much about her, but now I feel like I want to get to know her. She was only a teenager when . . . well, when she disappeared. And now that Nana Rose has sent me her diary—I mean, I think it's a diary, but—"

"Don't worry," Hannah said quickly. "Sophie speaks German. Come on over and she can read it. You'll be able to figure everything out."

Charlie wrapped the old green notebook in newspaper and placed it inside her backpack along with the red binder. What smelled so bad? Oh, gross—yesterday's tuna sandwich was stuck to the bottom. Charlie threw out the sandwich, but the backpack still smelled terrible. She slung it over one shoulder, put on her helmet, and hopped on her bike.

A strong breeze made the September air chilly, but Charlie didn't mind. Her favorite Hanukkah present last year was her new bike; she loved the freedom of racing around the neighborhood to hang out with friends.

Charlie gripped the brakes and slowed down as she approached the brown shingle house on the corner one block before Hannah's street. The house was small and shabby, with ugly strips of gray paint peeling from the windows. A few pink roses bloomed in front. Charlie was always careful when she passed by the house because a mean dog with densely corded black fur that hung over his eyes lived there. His owner was an older man who rarely came outside.

Jake called the dog Satan. It wasn't his real name, of course, but everyone in the neighborhood avoided him. Charlie loved most animals, and she would never admit this to anyone, but she was secretly a bit fearful around dogs, especially aggressive shaggy dogs with bad reputations for chasing kids and delivery people.

As Charlie scanned the yard, a car pulled up to the curb beside her and honked twice. She looked over to see that Devin McCarthy was sitting in the backseat. Charlie stopped breathing for a second while she slowly pedaled. Devin was the best cello player in the seventh grade. He had green eyes and thick brown hair that covered his ears.

Devin was kind of cute, but he knew he was the top cellist and managed to show off in a million little ways, like *always* playing in exact time and with precise intonation—even though he acted like he wasn't even trying. While most players needed Mr. Fernandez's help tuning up, Devin had perfect pitch and was especially good with tuning pegs; he would quickly tune his own cello, and then while he was waiting, launch into a solo piece that was usually two exercise books ahead of everyone else.

For the most part, Devin didn't say much. Sarah had always thought he might be shy, but Charlie figured Devin was more likely stuck on himself. Still, she couldn't deny that Devin was a natural musician; besides hitting every note with precision, Devin was the only kid who played like he was having a conversation, as if the music was a language he understood. Charlie was sure he'd be a professional cellist someday.

Devin's father waved from the driver's seat, and Charlie wondered if Devin would put down the window. Her throat felt weirdly tight. What would she say if he spoke? But the car quickly swerved around her and picked up speed. Devin hadn't even looked up.

Suddenly, Charlie heard a ferocious growl. From the corner of her eye she caught sight of a black ball of fur heading straight toward her. Charlie slammed on the brakes to avoid

28

striking the dog, but her front tire hit a rock, and with a hard jolt, she flew over the handlebars and crashed on the ground.

It took a minute for Charlie to catch her breath and force open her eyes. She wiggled her hands and feet, then rolled forward. There were ugly scrapes on both elbows, but nothing seemed broken. The bike lay a few feet away, and right next to it, her backpack. But before Charlie had a chance to get up, she heard a piercing yelp. Satan was sniffing and pawing at the backpack. He grabbed it between his teeth and raced away across the yard.

"No! *Stop!*" Charlie pushed herself up and sprinted after the dog. "Give that back to me!"

Satan ran around the house and ducked under the bushes. He was growling and snarling with the backpack firmly in his teeth. With a wild snort, he began to furiously shake the bag.

Charlie dove into the bushes after him, numb with fear that it would be too late; Lottie's notebook would be torn to shreds! She managed to grab the backpack by one strap and yanked with all her might. The bushes scratched against her face and arms, but she wouldn't let go. Satan planted his paws in the loose dirt at the edge of the flower bed. The harder Charlie pulled, the harder the dog hung on.

"What is this? What are you doing in my yard?" The owner appeared out of nowhere. He was tall and slightly bent, with a heavily lined face and a small tuft of gray hair at the top of his forehead. He had a deep voice and spoke with a formal, old-fashioned lilt—a little like Nana Rose, Charlie thought.

"Your dog took my bag! It has something important inside. I have to get it back!" Charlie exclaimed.

"Kinga!" The man shook his head and hurried toward the bushes. He pushed aside a branch and grasped the dog by the collar. "Bad dog! *Nem!* Give me that, you rascal!" The man raised the dog's head, forcing it to drop the backpack. Charlie fell backward with the bag in her lap.

Jagged tooth marks and small holes pierced the bottom of the backpack. Charlie's heart thudded against her ribs as she felt inside for Lottie's notebook. Still in one piece! She let out a long, exhausted moan as she brushed leaves and twigs from her clothing.

Then she eyed the beast suspiciously. "What kind of dog is that?" It had to be some sort of wild guard dog.

"Kinga is a Puli. Her breed is Hungarian." The man stiffly reached forward to help Charlie up.

"Puli? I've never seen a dog like that before." Charlie frowned, her arms wrapped tightly around the backpack. She hadn't expected the nasty dog to be a girl.

"They are common in Hungary. They are used for herding sheep.... You are not hurt, I see?" the man added without smiling.

"No, I'm okay, I guess."

The owner's lips were thin and pressed tightly together like two worms. His eyes were narrow and hooded. He didn't respond or look at all friendly.

"I'm Charlie Roth," she finally offered. "I live over there." She pointed toward the street behind them.

"Dr. Szemere." The man nodded slightly, holding fast to the dog's collar. "Kinga does not care to be teased by children. You must keep your bicycle on the road, young lady." He turned and started to walk toward the house.

"Excuse me," Charlie called after him.

Dr. Szemere stopped and turned halfway around.

"Are you Hungarian, too?" Charlie asked.

"That is correct." Dr. Szemere tilted his head to one side as if he was curious, but still did not smile. "Is there a reason that you ask?"

"N-no, not exactly. I guess I'd better leave now." Charlie coughed.

"Yes, you ought to be on your way." Dr. Szemere went into the house, with Kinga, tail between her legs, following him.

Charlie opened the backpack and pulled out the red project binder. The third page was titled *Lottie in Budapest,* and underneath, Charlie had already listed several famous musicians from Hungary she'd found online.

With a quick nod, she scribbled a note and circled it twice: *Kinga is Hungarian.*

CHAPTER SIX

"That crazy dog up the street took my backpack!" Charlie pointed at the ragged holes as Hannah opened the screen door to her house. "I met the dog's owner—that guy is *sca-ry!*"

Hannah pulled Charlie inside. "My parents know Dr. Szemere. He used to work at the hospital, but he's retired now."

"Well, his dog almost bit off my arm, and he didn't seem to care." Charlie removed her helmet and checked the bruises on her knees.

"Dad says he got a little strange after his wife passed away." Hannah frowned. "Mrs. Szemere was really nice, though. I remember she brought us roses from their garden."

The girls went down to the basement playroom, where Sophie was busy picking up toys while Hannah's baby sister napped. Sophie was the coolest au pair in Connecticut. She had spiked lavender hair and wore brass-studded boots. Her left eyebrow was pierced twice.

When Charlie handed her Lottie's notebook, she opened it with a long silver fingernail and glanced at the first page. "Ah yes, I can see that this is old." Sophie spoke English in a sing-song voice; every word sounded distinct and interesting.

Charlie's heart was thumping. What would the notebook reveal?

After studying the yellowed pages, Sophie flipped to the back, returned to the middle, and ran her fingers through her hair.

"What does it say?" Charlie sat up on her knees.

"I'm afraid I cannot read this so well," Sophie answered slowly. "You know, it is very old-fashioned, this script—it is difficult to understand. I've seen something like it with my granny."

"Can't you tell us anything?" Hannah asked. "Is it a diary?"

"I don't know," Sophie replied. "I can only make out a few of the words. This one says *nacht* . . . that means night."

"What else?" Hannah asked.

"Well, here, I believe this says *Mo-zart* . . ."

"Mozart?" Charlie repeated.

"Why would she be writing about Mozart?" Hannah frowned.

"Lottie played the violin. She was studying music." Charlie dropped from her knees to the floor. "Maybe she had to learn a Mozart piece for her lessons."

"I am terribly sorry," Sophie said, "but I can't read much else—just some dates. Here it is written August, and here, September. Otherwise, I cannot be certain. You need an older person, someone very old perhaps, to read this." She scratched her eyebrow above the gold rings, and Charlie's brow felt itchy, too.

"Wait," Sophie said suddenly. "I think this is again a name; yes, it is a name."

"What name?" the girls asked in unison.

"Here I see *Nathan*—yes, I am sure it is Nathan—Nathan Kul-ka."

"Kulka!" Charlie exclaimed. "That was Lottie's last name, too."

"Perhaps she had a brother?" Sophie suggested.

"No, there were only two sisters." Charlie shook her head.

"Then who could it be?" Hannah asked.

"I don't know," Charlie replied. "But I'm going to find out."

Sophie closed the notebook and handed it back to Charlie. "This relative of yours, the one who made the book—did she come to live with your family in America?"

"Lottie never..." Charlie faltered. "Lottie's sister—my nana—came to America on a ship with her mother, but she wasn't with them. Lottie got lost—or we think she—I mean, she disappeared..." Charlie's voice trailed off. "...during the Holocaust."

A deep furrow set in between Sophie's eyes. "I am so sorry to hear this. How horrible! We learned about this history at school, of course, but in Zurich, I didn't know anyone who lost a family member like that."

When Charlie got home, Mom was cooking pasta for dinner. "Any luck?"

"Sophie couldn't read the diary." Charlie shook her head. "She could only make out a few words. She said the old-fashioned script was too hard."

"I'm sorry." Mom sighed.

"It's okay. Nana can tell me more when we see her. I was just hoping I wouldn't have to wait until then." Charlie took out dishes to set the table. "I might have gotten a clue, though. Sophie made out a name in the notebook—Nathan Kulka. Do you know who that is?"

"I don't know anyone named Nathan. Maybe a cousin?" Mom thought for a minute while she stirred the pasta. "Another question for Nana when we visit."

Charlie and Mom were going to Florida the following Friday. Mom was letting her leave school a little early—right after orchestra auditions, Charlie thought with a silent gulp.

"It'll be a nice visit for just us girls, don't you think?" Mom smiled. "We'll have plenty of time to talk over the weekend."

Charlie nodded. Jake couldn't miss preseason basketball, and Dad was in the middle of a trial, so it was only going to be Charlie and Mom visiting Nana this time.

Charlie hesitated. "There's something else. . . ."

Mom looked up, waiting.

"Sophie seemed surprised that we had someone in our family who was lost in the Holocaust. She said it was something she learned about in history class. But it was like none of it seemed real to her until now . . . I mean, until she met someone with a relative like Lottie."

"Oh, I see." Mom had that vague, you're-too-young-to-understand-this look on her face. "Well, the Holocaust occurred long before Sophie was born, and I suppose, even when truly terrible events happen—after many years, sometimes people forget exactly how real they were."

"The thing is, Mom, I want to *find* Lottie—I don't want her to be forgotten!"

Mom put down the spoon and smoothed a curl from Charlie's cheek. "Just keep on going. I think you *are* finding Lottie—as best anyone could."

CHAPTER SEVEN

Charlie lay in bed that night, totally exhausted. Even texting Sarah felt like an effort: **Sophie couldn't translate Lottie's diary. The German script was too old-fashioned. She said maybe an older person could do it.**

Isn't Amy Klein's nana German??? Sarah texted back. **She is definitely old!**

Sarah was always right. Amy's grandmother was from Germany and had recently moved in with them. Charlie recalled that Amy had raised her hand when their Hebrew school teacher asked which students had family members who died in the Shoah.

Charlie texted Amy before turning out the lights. She stared at the dark ceiling, trying to sleep, but her mind wouldn't stop jumping between thoughts of Lottie and worrying about her orchestra audition.

What would it be like to play with a symphony in front of hundreds of people? Once in a while, Mr. Fernandez would perform a solo for them. Charlie loved watching his expression, his face transfixed and his eyes fluttering as he swayed to the music. Sometimes it didn't seem like he was even in the room.

Mr. Fernandez had a beautiful wooden bow decorated with inlaid mother-of-pearl. It dipped and floated on the strings, the sound waning, then soaring. Had Lottie played like that? Immersed in the music like she was part of the sound?

When Charlie finally fell asleep, she had the strangest dream. It was the middle of orchestra rehearsal, and Mr. Fernandez had just pointed out to his new assistant, Ms. Patel, how superbly Devin did vibrato on the cello. It was Charlie's turn to play, but she couldn't read a single note. The noteheads and stems began to separate from the staff and dance across the sheet music, refusing to stay still; Charlie couldn't follow them.

Just as she was about to burst into tears, Charlie thought she heard the soft refrain of one of her favorite Beethoven sonatas. She turned her head toward the music, and there was Lottie, wearing a long linen dress and a yellow straw hat. She was holding a finely carved violin with a maple flame across its back.

Lottie lifted the instrument and began to play. Everyone stopped to listen. Devin's jaw dropped as Lottie stood on her tiptoes, did a pirouette, and played the most difficult section without missing one note.

When she was done, Lottie handed Charlie her instrument—it was light as a feather. Suddenly, Charlie could play the piece perfectly, too. Mr. Fernandez was beaming, and Devin's mouth hung open. But when Charlie finished and tried to give the violin back to Lottie, she simply floated away. All that was left was her straw hat, lying carelessly on the floor.

Charlie's eyes opened. Shivering, she glanced at the alarm clock—6 a.m. She rolled back on her stomach and buried her face in the pillow, but it was no use, her eyelids wouldn't stay shut. Slipping out of bed, she silently crept down the stairs to the family room. Thin daylight streamed through the blinds, casting shadows across the couch and coffee table. Charlie pulled the photograph album from the shelf and flipped through its pages until she found the picture of Lottie with her violin.

Dad's magnifying glass was lying on the coffee table. Peering through it, she could see Lottie's dimples clearly. Mom was right, they did look alike! What was that around her neck? Charlie hadn't noticed it before, but Lottie was wearing a necklace with a small pendant. Charlie hesitated for a moment, then pulled the picture from the album and hurried back upstairs to her room. She pinned the photograph on the bulletin board above her desk and studied it for a long while.

"What happened to you?" Charlie finally whispered. "Did you find a safe place to hide?"

She traced the length of Lottie's violin with the tip of her finger. "I love playing violin, too, you know. My bowing technique is solid, and I have the best rhythm in the orchestra. I practice every day. We have orchestra auditions next Friday morning—a week from today. I think if I try super hard, I have a shot at making concertmaster." Nana Rose would come visit and watch her perform. She would be so proud and excited to see her granddaughter at the front of the orchestra—nothing would make Nana happier. Charlie leaned back and smiled.

And wouldn't Devin be surprised!

Before getting dressed for school, Charlie took one last look at Lottie's photo. "I am going to find you. I promise, I will."

CHAPTER EIGHT

When Charlie checked her phone after math class later that day, there was a text waiting from Sarah: **Didn't your nana arrive by ship? Have you Googled Ellis Island? We found Poppa Antonio there.**

Good idea, will do!! Charlie texted back.

As soon as Charlie got home from school, she opened her laptop and found the website. Charlie's class had gone on a field trip to Ellis Island in fifth grade, and now she wished she'd paid more attention. She remembered that the huge hall where many thousands of immigrants had arrived in America seemed like an abandoned train station, cold and gray. Charlie and Sarah had spent most of their time chatting with Amy and Hannah and listening to their voices echo in the enormous room.

What if Lottie had found her way to America all alone?

How would she feel standing by herself in that giant hall—a girl who spoke no English and had no family there to help her? Charlie wondered whether Lottie would even be allowed to enter the United States—didn't the guide say that many people—sick people, people without the right papers—were turned back?

The Ellis Island archive was simple to use. There was a place to search passenger ship records, so Charlie quickly typed in *Charlotte Kulka*. She left the date blank and held her breath.

In a flash, a screen appeared with a few names that might have matched, but none from the right time and country. When she tried *Lottie Kulka* only one match appeared—from a ship that arrived in the 1800s.

No luck, Charlie texted Sarah. **I couldn't find Lottie at Ellis Island.**

Maybe she changed her name? Sarah asked.

Sarah had a point. Charlie suddenly recalled that the Ellis Island guide had talked about that being common. Lots of people had chosen or been given new names when they reached America. Sometimes the clerk taking down the information simply didn't understand or misspelled foreign-sounding names. What if Lottie Kulka had become Lottie Cohen or Lottie Katz or Lottie Smith? How would Charlie ever find her?

Another text from Sarah appeared: **Any other relatives?**

"Mom!" Charlie called at the top of her lungs, but no one answered. Then she remembered that Mom was out with

a client. **What was Nana's mother's name?** she texted her mother. **Need it for my research.**

A minute later Charlie's phone buzzed: **Aurelie Kulka. Good luck!**

Charlie typed in the names *Rose* and *Aurelie Kulka*. There it was! Aurelie Kulka, age forty-six, on the ship the *Fräulein Hilda*, and next to it, an entry for her daughter, Rose. How strange to picture Nana Rose as a child on the boat to America; how would Nana have felt coming into New York Harbor and seeing the Statue of Liberty for the first time?

And what about the mysterious Nathan Kulka from Lottie's diary? Charlie carefully typed in the name *Kulka* and left the other information blank. She swallowed hard. A new list came up with other names, including Magda, Herman, Erwin, Valerie, and N. Kulka. Charlie stared at the screen, wondering whether *N.* could be *Nathan*.

Found Nana's ship!!! Charlie texted Sarah.

Yay!! Sarah replied.

"Dinner!" Charlie jumped as Jake banged the door open. "Didn't you hear me yelling? Mom said she'd be late and Dad's at the gym, so I took the liberty of making us some excellent burgers."

"How many times do I have to tell you that I'm a vegetarian, Jake?"

"Too bad! Wait till you see how thick and juicy I made yours—and you'd better eat every bite." Jake loudly licked his fingers. "But...if you *really* want, I could make you grilled cheese—"

"Hey, yeah, thanks, that'd be—"

"—with yummy bits of corned beef, of course."

Trying not to smile, Charlie growled and pushed Jake out the door. "I'll make myself a salad later. Go away!" With a sly grin, she sent one last text to Sarah: **Brothers, ugh!! SO annoying!**

Charlie's phone buzzed again; it was Amy this time: **My nana says she can read the old German. Come right over!**

With an excited *"Yes!"* Charlie carefully packed up Lottie's notebook and headed for her bike.

CHAPTER NINE

"Hi, Charlie, come on in." Amy's mom answered the door with a worried look on her face. "I'm afraid my mother is a bit tuckered out today. I'm not sure whether she's entirely up to this." Mrs. Klein's foot tapped rapidly on the stone floor of the foyer as she glanced back and forth behind her.

A white-haired lady with enormous tortoiseshell glasses hobbled into the front hall. She was puffing and leaning heavily on a walker. Amy stood beside her, holding her steady.

"You remember Charlie Roth from down the street, Mother?" Mrs. Klein asked.

"Yes, of course, such a sweet girl." Nana Klein inspected Charlie through thick lenses.

"There's something in German that she needs translated. Some sort of diary from a great-aunt," Mrs. Klein explained.

"It was from my nana's older sister, Charlotte—but

everyone called her Lottie." Charlie carefully lifted the worn leather notebook from her backpack.

"Of course I can assist!" Nana Klein waved one thin arm as she supported herself above the walker. "Don't worry, my angel granddaughter here told me all about your auntie's diary, poor girl!" She grasped Amy's arm and leaned closer to Charlie: "You know, I lost my parents too in the Shoah—and all four brothers, may they rest in peace." Nana Klein pulled an embroidered handkerchief from the sleeve of her blouse and blew her nose.

Charlie shivered and took a deep breath. "I was named after her, but we don't really know what happened to Lottie once she disappeared."

Nana Klein motioned for Amy and Charlie to sit beside her on the couch, while Mrs. Klein went to make the girls some tea.

"Now we shall see what we can find out about this relative, your great-aunt Lottie." Nana Klein smoothed the front of her blouse and with one shaky hand took the green notebook and opened it to the first page. "Aha! The old script, no wonder a young person couldn't read it."

Nana Klein's white head bobbed slowly as she turned the pages. The girls looked at each other with raised eyebrows. Charlie sat on her fingers, trying not to fidget.

After carefully closing the notebook, Nana Klein inched closer to Charlie and lightly touched her knee. "Your auntie was a great music lover, am I right?"

"Yes. Lottie played the violin," Charlie responded.

"Is it a diary, Nana? What does it say?" Amy asked.

"My darlings," Nana Klein replied. "You know how you girls have your rock-and-roll music and rapping, in concerts and on television? All that noise, *oy!*"

"What?" Charlie and Hannah stared at each other.

"Rock music! The type my granddaughter here listens to all the time, too loud, so it's going to ruin her ears?"

"Nana, what does that have to do with Lottie's notebook?" Amy asked.

"Well, in Europe, before the war, we had our popular music, too—opera and symphonies. Why, when I was a young girl, I had a little book just like this one." Nana Klein clapped her hands together. "My goodness, I had almost forgotten."

"But what is it?" Charlie asked. "What does the notebook say?"

"It's a music journal," Nana Klein replied simply. "Your relative, here is her given name, as you said, Charlotte—she went to the symphony, to the opera, and she wrote down all the music that she saw and heard. This is Mozart's *The Magic Flute*—oh, she liked that one, she saw it three times!"

"You're kidding!" Hannah exclaimed. "A *music* journal was her most prized possession?"

"Oh yes, I can imagine it," Nana Klein replied. "In those days, the opera singers, they were like rock stars, like gods to us. Look, she saw the famous tenor, Wilhelm Anton Volkmann. I watched him perform, too—he was so dramatic! So exciting! All my friends were wild for him, I can assure you."

Nana Klein picked up the journal and flipped through the pages. "You see how each symphony is noted, each opera, and where she sat—although mostly, your great-aunt watched and listened from the standing section. The opera was beastly expensive, so I used to do the same. We stood at the back, and it cost very little. I was young and strong then, like you!"

Nana Klein began to cough. Charlie looked at her wrinkled hands and white hair, and wondered what color it was when she was younger.

"What's this column?" Charlie pointed to a list on the right side of each page.

"Those are the names of her family and friends, the ones she went to hear the music with—here you can see *Mutti*—that's 'Mother,' and on the next line, a gentleman named Nathan Kulka."

"We haven't figured out who he is yet," Charlie said. "Maybe a cousin."

"Over here, I see a name that is repeated." Nana Klein slowly traced one bony finger along the edge of the notebook. "I need more light, please." The girls jumped up and together pulled a large lamp closer. "Ah," said Nana Klein, "much better. Yes, here is the name—*Johann*—Johann Schmidt. He appears several times at the end of the journal. The last entry, the final symphony—she attended with her Mr. Schmidt."

"I wonder who he was," Charlie said.

"Perhaps a young man...or a family friend? He doesn't

sound Jewish! How old was she when she wrote this journal?" Nana Klein asked.

"She was a teenager," Charlie replied.

"So, a young man, then," Nana Klein said with a knowing smile. "Apparently the two young people went to a concert together—and then the book ends." Nana Klein removed her glasses and rubbed her eyes.

"Nothing else?" Amy bent forward.

"*Nein*, nothing." Nana Klein shrugged. "Nineteen thirty-eight was the year of *Kristallnacht*—the terrifying 'Night of Broken Glass,' when Jews were attacked and synagogues destroyed. After the Nazis invaded Austria, many other countries followed. It was the end of life as we knew it." She turned away and cleared her throat.

Charlie reached over and gently hugged Nana Klein's stooped shoulders. "Thank you for reading Lottie's journal for me. I am very, very sorry about your family."

Nana Klein folded her hands over her heart. "I live on for them in my old age. On Yom Kippur I light a yahrzeit candle for my dear brothers." She looked lovingly at Amy, who returned her soft smile. "And I see them in my granddaughter's beautiful eyes."

CHAPTER TEN

Dear Nana Rose,

I hope you like the enclosed photo; it's me playing the violin in the school orchestra last year. If I work hard enough, I think I have a chance of being concertmaster this year. Someday, I hope that I might be able to play as well as Lottie! Thank you for sending me her music journal. I want to talk to you about it when we see you next weekend, and I promise to always keep it in a safe place.

Lots of love, xox,

Charlie

PS—Did Lottie have a boyfriend?

PPS—Can you tell me who Nathan Kulka was?

Charlie twisted her hair into a ponytail on top of her head. She stood in front of the mirror, holding her violin at right angles to her body. Turning sideways, she analyzed her posture, then arched her back and stood even straighter. She began warming up with an easy scale and then moved on to more challenging pieces. At first, every note was in time with the metronome. But when Charlie tried to practice pizzicato...snap! A string broke loose on the second pluck. It dangled over the side of the violin like a fishing line.

"Oh no!" Charlie exclaimed.

"What's wrong—what happened?" Jake hollered from his bedroom.

"Nothing! I'm fine!" Charlie kicked the floor with her heel.

It was pointless to continue—Mr. Fernandez would have to replace the string at school. Charlie bit her lip and pulled the rubber band from her hair, letting her strawberry curls fall over her shoulders. The broken string suddenly seemed like a bad omen. How much of a shot did she *really* have at concertmaster this year? Yes, she loved being in the orchestra. She was a strong player, and she'd been practicing a lot. But was she honestly ready? Her intonation wasn't flawless, her vibrato was only so-so, and her sight reading still needed work.

Tommy Lee could sight-read anything, even with his eyes half shut. Or maybe he was playing every single piece by heart? Was that possible?

Charlie sat on the bed and picked up the red project binder. Now the pages seemed as empty as her chances of being concertmaster. Lottie's diary was nothing more than a music journal. The Ellis Island search confirmed that Nana Rose had come to the United States, but Charlie already knew that. She was no closer to actually *finding* Lottie.

"Time for pancakes!" Charlie looked up to see Dad standing at her bedroom door. Charlie and Dad always made chocolate pancakes together on Saturday mornings; it had been a tradition between them ever since she was little.

"I'm really tired, Daddy; can't you make them without me?"

"Are you kidding? You're the only one who knows exactly how many chocolate chips to add." Dad sat down at the edge of the bed and rubbed the bald spot in his speckled hair. His crystal-blue eyes searched hers with concern. "What's wrong?"

"Nothing," Charlie mumbled.

Jake poked his head in. "Charlie's just upset because orchestra auditions are coming up soon. I don't know why she's freaking out and making such a big deal about it, though. Seventh graders almost never make concertmaster."

"What do you know about any of this?" Charlie shot back. "The only instrument you've ever tried is the harmonica!"

"Yeah, but I heard it from a girl who plays bass." Jake grinned like he knew the girl pretty well.

"Oh, you mean the blond girl with the braids who's always picking you up in her car?" Charlie raised one eyebrow.

"Uh...maybe?" Jake's face got a little red as he pretended to cough.

"Listen, Jake—I think Mom needs you downstairs," Dad said. "She said something about fudge donuts."

Jake shook his head. "Okay, I can take a hint. And a bribe.

But Dad, please do this whole family a favor and tell Charlie she needs to relax."

Dad waited until they could hear Jake's footsteps on the stairs before speaking again.

"Is Jake right? Are you worried about your audition?"

"No, I'm fine," Charlie began. "Except that Devin McCarthy's in seventh grade, and I bet he'll make first chair for cellos, but I probably won't even be in the first *section* for violins, and I'm sure Tommy Lee will be showing Mr. Fernandez all his impressive skills at *his* audition, and . . ."

"And?" Dad said gently.

Charlie simply shrugged.

Dad glanced at the red binder sitting on her bed. "How is your research project going? Tell me what you've learned so far about Nana's sister."

Charlie pulled forward, hugging her knees. "That's another problem, Dad. Nana Rose sent me Lottie's notebook, and I thought it would tell me something new about her, but it turned out there was nothing in it except a list of concerts she went to with different people. I checked Ellis Island, and I found Nana Rose, her mom, and some other names . . . but nothing that seems to be leading anywhere." Charlie slid off the bed and returned with a tissue to dab her nose.

"One way or the other, Charlie, I'm sure your teacher will appreciate all your diligence and hard work." Dad patted her shoulder.

"That's not the point, though—not really," Charlie replied.

"I mean, yeah, I want a good grade, but mostly, I want to find out something important about Lottie. Something *solid*." There was a long silence while she stared at the crumpled tissue. "Dad, all those people—our family in the photo album, the children, even babies—they died because…just because they were Jewish. Nana Rose was only a little girl when her father was killed, and she could have been killed, too." Charlie's eyes were suddenly full.

"Yes." Dad took Charlie's hand. "That's true."

"Nana Rose has lived her whole life *not knowing* what actually happened to her sister! I want to find Lottie. Not just for school, but for Nana and our family. But the thing is, what if I can't? What if Jake was right that I won't find anything because—well, what if it's because…"

"Because she died in the Holocaust like the others?" Dad asked softly.

Charlie nodded; her eyes were streaming now, and she could barely swallow. After another silence, she said, "I want to be the best at violin, Dad. I want Nana Rose to be as proud of me as she was of her sister. But I'm not even a sure thing for *concertmaster* at school. Lottie played with the *Vienna Philharmonic* when she was barely older than I am!"

"Come over here." Dad pulled Charlie into his warm arms. "Your nana could not be more proud of her beautiful, talented granddaughter; she loves you just as you are. And listen to me—you don't have to rush your life, Charlie; all the good stuff will come in its own time, when you're ready for each and every challenge."

Charlie swallowed hard and silently nodded. When she looked up at Dad's face, she was shocked to see that the corners of his eyes were damp, too.

CHAPTER ELEVEN

The following Wednesday morning, Charlie woke up with the opening theme from Beethoven's Fifth Symphony, "Ta-ta-ta-dum, ta-ta-ta-dum," stuck in her head. She hummed the first few bars while she got dressed, packed her backpack, grabbed her violin—and waited for the bus to school.

Orchestra class was first period on Wednesdays, and today was the final group rehearsal before auditions. Not every kid liked starting the day with music class, but Charlie couldn't help but happily swing her violin case on her way past the math and science wing before heading to the rehearsal room below the auditorium. Hillmont Middle School was a modern steel-and-glass building, but Charlie liked the way the orchestra room somehow seemed old, with its low acoustic tile ceilings and wooden cubbies teeming with instruments. The air was always tinged with the scent of rosin, a pungent pine.

To Charlie, the rehearsal space was as cozy as her family room at home. The chairs and metal stands nearly touched each other, and countless piles of sheet music covered every available surface. In the background before rehearsals began, there was always the low buzz of instruments being tuned. Whenever Mr. Fernandez eventually raised his baton, Charlie felt a calm sense of focus wash over her. She loved watching him conduct from the podium, guiding the tempo and dynamics with his baton, facial expressions, and gestures—especially when he opened his arms wider and wider for the music to build to the top of a crescendo.

The orchestra was like a puzzle—fitting melody with harmony, keeping bows in sync. It was as much about teamwork as Jake's basketball team passing the ball back and forth down the court, with the players carefully positioning themselves in order to score.

Charlie found a spot in the middle of the first violin section and briefly eyed the chair closest to the podium—the concertmaster's seat.

As if on cue, Tommy Lee immediately plunked down in front of Charlie and yawned as he took out his instrument and began to tune. Tommy was tall and had spiked black hair so full that it nearly blocked Charlie's view. She had to lean sideways to see around him.

All of a sudden, she noticed a girl with a French braid and wire-rimmed glasses working with Mr. Fernandez in the viola section. Charlie did a double take. For a split second, she thought the girl was Sarah. But it was only a sixth grader who'd recently moved from Texas. She was having so much trouble with her fingering that Mr. Fernandez had to place extra blue stickers on the neck of her instrument. He patiently showed her again and again where to press each finger. When she finally got it right, Mr. Fernandez seemed even more excited than the girl, Charlie thought.

Charlie glanced around the rest of the room, hoping to find someone to exchange smiles with as she tuned her violin, but nobody looked her way.

It was getting late, and Mr. Fernandez stepped onto the podium, but a few seats remained empty. Devin was still nowhere in sight. Where was he? How could he miss the final rehearsal before auditions—was he that sure of himself? A short, freckled boy Charlie knew vaguely from gym class arrived and took the seat beside her. He grunted hello and quietly stuck his gum under the chair before bending forward to tighten his bow.

Then the new girl from Texas dropped her viola with a loud thud, and a second later, everyone looked up when Devin finally walked into the room, headed straight for the front, and without a word, took the open chair at first stand as if he knew he belonged there.

Mr. Fernandez coughed loudly and knocked his foot against the podium. "Okay, people . . . are we ready at last? Let's start with *Eine kleine Nachtmusik*." He raised his baton and hesitated. "Pay close attention, the opening section's a little tricky. There are a couple of quick shifts at the beginning."

Charlie planted her feet, back straight, bow ready—she'd practiced that part last night for twenty minutes at least.

Mr. Fernandez lowered his baton and scratched his ear. "Actually... perhaps we could have one of the violins demonstrate first?" He glanced at Tommy, who raised his chin and started to rise from his chair.

"Ms. Roth?" Mr. Fernandez turned his gaze past Tommy and gestured. "Would you please stand up and show us? Start with the third measure."

Charlie sprang to her feet, accidentally knocking the back of Tommy's chair with a sharp jolt. But then she stood tall, arched her back, and played with smooth shifts, hitting nearly every note with a clear, true sound.

"Excellent! You've been practicing, and it shows." Mr. Fernandez applauded. "And that's precisely what everyone else needs to do. Go home tonight and practice this section at least five times until it sounds easy—exactly the way Charlie played it."

Charlie tried hard to stifle the smile bursting from her lips. She could see Tommy's shoulders stiffen in reaction to Mr. Fernandez's praise. When he stood at the end of rehearsal, he didn't speak a word to anyone and packed up his violin quickly.

"Auditions are on Friday morning starting at eleven a.m.," Ms. Patel reminded them. "You already have your assigned time slots during lunch period. Please be prompt."

"And don't forget, everyone—how do you get to Carnegie Hall? Practice! Practice! Practice!" Mr. Fernandez chuckled to himself as Ms. Patel clapped cheerfully, and the students filed out of the room.

Charlie was walking through the door when Devin caught up from behind. "Nice work," he mumbled.

Was Devin being sarcastic? Charlie couldn't tell.

"To be honest, I was petrified," she replied. Devin gave her a curious look and then slipped past her into the hallway. Ugh, that was awkward. *Petrified?* Like an old tree stump?

At the end of the day, Charlie had an open study period with Hannah and Amy. After finishing their math homework, the girls started work on their family history projects. Hannah was having trouble with her research, too. She'd chosen her father's cousin, an older woman named Lian who'd been a student in Beijing during the Cultural Revolution. Lian's school had been shut by the army and the students had been forced to do manual labor. They lived under terrible conditions. Eventually, Lian was able to emigrate to the United States, leaving family and friends behind. When Hannah asked her to describe her experiences, however, she simply drew a blank. The only thing Lian recalled clearly was the sweet scent of cherry blossoms by the highway where they toiled.

Charlie was thinking how strong and brave Lian must have been when a series of loud thumps made her jump in her seat.

"Something wrong?" Amy asked.

"What's that drumming noise?" Charlie could hear "ta-ta-ta-dum"—the very same "ta-ta-ta-dum"—that had been stuck in the back of her head all day—except now it sounded as if the Fifth Symphony was being tapped on a desk.

"Oh, that's just Devin." Hannah giggled. "He's sitting a couple of tables behind you. He always does that!"

"Devin McCarthy?" Charlie's eyebrows lifted.

"What other Devin is there?" Hannah asked. "He's in my social studies class this year. Doesn't he play an instrument?"

"Devin doesn't just play an instrument..." Charlie whispered. "He's the best cellist in the orchestra. The problem is, he knows it."

"That sounds about right." Hannah laughed. "Because he's like a boy genius in social studies, too. I heard he's already finished ten pages of his family history report even though the whole project is only supposed to be eight pages long—including exhibits!"

"Look at the huge book he's reading." Amy grinned at Charlie.

Charlie turned her head over her shoulder just as Devin glanced up from a thick volume. She could see the title, *Companion to Irish Traditional Music*. He quickly closed the book, grabbed his backpack, and hurried over to the water fountain.

"Hey." Hannah looked at her watch. "My dad's taking me to get new cleats after school. Do you guys want to come?"

"Can't," Amy replied. "Science club meeting. Thanks, though."

"I probably shouldn't, either." Charlie sighed. "I have to

practice for my audition. And I should start packing for Florida. Mom and I are going to see Nana Rose this weekend."

"Oh, that's great!" Amy flashed thumbs up. "You'll finally get to talk to her about your great-aunt Lottie and your project."

The minute she got on the bus, Charlie texted Sarah: **Mr. Fernandez asked me to play solo this morning. It was pretty cool.** After a pause, she added, **But orchestra is still awful without you! Devin is driving me crazy.**

What'd he do? Sarah texted right back.

Nothing, I guess. Charlie crinkled her nose. **Except that he's always so sure of himself!**

Sarah replied with two smiley faces and an exclamation point in bold.

When Charlie got home from school, a letter from Nana Rose was waiting on her desk.

My dearest Charlie,

I am filled with happiness to receive your letter and know that you will keep Lottie's journal safe. We all loved music in our family! I remember when I was small, I was envious that Lottie would get dressed up with an elegant hat and lace gloves and go to the opera. My mother's favorite aunt gave Lottie opera glasses made of silver. Then Mutti let her wear a bit of rouge. How glamorous Lottie seemed to me, how grown-up!

Of course, times were very hard in Vienna. My father was a

professor of mathematics at the university, but because we were Jewish, he lost his position. We moved to a simple apartment that had no bath of its own—only one tub in the attic for the building to share. I remember how cold it was up there; I was always shivering! Lottie and I slept together in the salon, where we also ate. It was our dining room/living room/bedroom. But this I loved because my sister would talk to me at night before sleep—usually, about concerts and music. We all hoped that someday Lottie would be a famous soloist, and my dear parents saved every extra penny for her lessons.

You have asked about Nathan. My father had a second or maybe third cousin; his name was Morris Kulka. He was a dentist, and married to a kind woman named Eva. They had a son called Nathan, who was studying to be a dentist, like the father. These cousins lived in Hungary, in a small village outside of Budapest. One time, they came to stay with us in Vienna for a few days, when times were better. Lottie and Nathan became good friends during that visit and went to a concert with the grown-ups. I was not so happy then, you see, because they left me behind. Nathan played the violin, too, or maybe the viola.

We saw these cousins only once or twice, and then of course came the war. Morris and Eva were taken away to the camps, but I do not know what happened to Nathan.

I have to tell you, dear Charlie, I have wondered sometimes whether Nathan did survive. Once, many years ago when your grandfather Sam was still living, we were passing through Bridgeport, Connecticut, and I saw a sign for a dentist. The name on the sign was Dr. N. Kulka. But we did not stop. I must be honest, *it was too painful to even hope that it might be Cousin Nathan, whom I had last seen when I was a small child—and anyway, we were going someplace in a great hurry. Of course, there must be very many Dr. Kulkas in America; it was probably somebody else.*

Did my sister have a special boyfriend? My darling Charlie, I do not know. We were not, as you might imagine, free to go out like teenagers today, but on the other hand, the birds and the bees were not invented by your generation! I can only tell you that Lottie was a beautiful girl, as you are, and that I am sure many young men admired her for her lovely spirit as well as her beauty.

I am tired now, but I hope that I have helped you. Of course, we can discuss this more when I see you very soon!

My love to you, Schnuckelpuss,
Nana Rose

Charlie read the letter twice and opened the red binder. At the top of a new page, she wrote *COUSIN NATHAN???* Then she texted Sarah: **We might have a cousin in Bridgeport! A dentist from Hungary.**

Sarah texted back instantly. **Awesome! So…what next??**

Charlie closed her eyes and held the phone tight for a second before responding: **So now—I'm going to try calling him!**

CHAPTER TWELVE

There were three Kulkas listed in Bridgeport. The first name was David Kulka, the second was Nat, and the third listing was simply N. Kulka. Charlie took a deep breath and locked her door. She tried the number for Nat first. Her heart was beating so loudly that she could hardly hear the dial tone.

"Hello?" A woman's voice answered.

"Hi, this is Charlie." Her voice croaked, oddly froglike. "Is there a Nathan—a Nathan Kulka who lives there, by any chance?"

"Nathan?" the lady repeated.

"Yes, I'm a relative—a cousin, kind of."

"No, there's no Nathan here, dearie. My sister's name is Natalie. You must have the wrong number."

"Oh." The phone clicked before Charlie had a chance to breathe.

Charlie tried N. Kulka next. The phone rang for several minutes, but nobody picked up. Was it worth trying David Kulka? There was no one in Lottie's music journal named David, but it couldn't hurt. Charlie went ahead and dialed the number. But again, no answer, not even a voice mail message.

What was she thinking? Even if the right Nathan Kulka had ever lived in Bridgeport, Grandpa Sam had passed away when Charlie was a baby—it must have been at least ten years since Nana Rose saw the dentist's sign, maybe more. What were the chances he would still be there?

Charlie slumped into her chair in frustration and glanced across the room at her violin case. She thought of all the times she and Nana Rose had sat together on her bed chatting about violin music and concerts. Nana Rose knew more about classical music than anyone Charlie had ever known, even Mr. Fernandez. And Nana was always so thoughtful and encouraging! Even now, though Nana had become a bit hard of hearing and sometimes mixed things up, she remained warm, cheerful, and full of helpful advice.

Nana Rose had almost never talked about the Holocaust with Charlie. But how awful it must have been for her to lose her sister! As much as Charlie detested Jake, she could not imagine her life without him.

Charlie picked up the phone again. "If at first you don't succeed, try, try again." Nana Rose was nearly as famous for her sayings as she was for her strudel, and this was one of her favorites.

Charlie dialed the number for N. Kulka once more. This time, a man responded.

"Hullo?" The man on the other end spoke in a thick voice. "Hullo? Who's on the line?"

"Oh, h-hi," Charlie sputtered. "I'm looking for Dr. Nathan Kulka—he's a dentist, or he might have been a dentist..."

"Nate's not here anymore. He retired a long time ago. I was his partner; you need somebody to look at your teeth? You've got a cavity, maybe?"

Charlie hesitated. "I was really hoping to find Dr. Kulka."

"Well, he's at the home," the man replied.

"What do you mean?"

"The seniors' home—you know, the one in Greenfield. Nate's in the Alzheimer's unit, I'm afraid. His mind has been affected—dementia."

"Are—are you sure?" Charlie asked.

"Yeah, yeah, he's been there two, maybe three years. Nate's no youngster anymore. None of us are. Anything else I can do for you?"

Charlie's mouth had gone dry. "Do you happen to know whether—oh, gosh, never mind!"

"All right, then." The phone clicked. Silence.

Charlie turned her head toward the bulletin board and Lottie's photo. Nathan Kulka was still alive and living in Greenfield. It was just two towns over on the highway.

"Cousin Nathan is half an hour away!" she whispered. "Maybe."

CHAPTER THIRTEEN

Charlie's knees bounced up and down as she searched online for seniors' housing in Greenfield. She quickly found the Connecticut Helping Home for Seniors.

"How may I assist you?" The woman answering her call had a voice that sounded official.

"Hello?" Charlie croaked. "I'm trying to . . . I'm looking for someone named Nathan Kulka; he's a dentist. Do you have someone by that—"

"Of course," the woman interrupted her. "Dr. Kulka is still here with us. I believe he's in his room—I'll put you through."

"Wait—you mean right away?" Charlie asked hoarsely.

"Hold on, this will only take a second."

"Hello?" A man's voice came on the line. "Who is this?"

"Hi." Charlie's voice squeaked.

"Who's there?" the man barked.

Charlie cleared her throat. "My name is Charlie Roth, and I was just wondering—"

"What did you say? Speak louder."

"I'm Charlie Roth, and I might be a relative of yours, maybe; a second cousin, sort of."

"A relative? What relative? I don't remember you!" the man exclaimed.

"I'm Charlie, my name is Charlie Roth—I'm related to Charlotte Kulka."

There was a long pause. "What are you saying? Speak up!" the man finally shouted.

"Do you come from Hungary?" Charlie asked.

"What are you asking? Who is this?"

"I'm a relative of *Lottie Kulka!*" Charlie yelled into the phone.

"Lottie who? Say it again?"

"Lottie Kulka! Lottie from Vienna!" Charlie drew three shallow breaths and waited.

Another silence and some crackling on the line. This was a mix-up, all a big mistake.

"Lottie Kulka?" The man's voice sounded broken, like gravel.

"Yes," Charlie replied.

"From Vienna?"

"Yes."

"Lottie Kulka is dead!"

The phone clicked, and the man was gone.

CHAPTER FOURTEEN

Charlie stepped back. She couldn't breathe. The phone buzzed, but she didn't answer. Now the buzzing wouldn't stop.

It was Sarah, texting: **Did you find your cousin? What did he say?**

Charlie typed the words slowly: **He said Lottie is dead.**

The phone instantly rang. "What happened?" Sarah exclaimed.

"I talked to this man who sounded like he was actually Cousin Nathan. But then he got completely muddled. He might have Alzheimer's."

"That's really bad." Sarah sighed. "My great-grandpa is like that—he can't always remember my name anymore. But listen, how do you know this guy is even your cousin? Maybe he was just confused about everything."

"I guess... except that he said Lottie was dead, exactly like he knew her."

"You have to go see him." Sarah had that can-do tone in her voice that Charlie missed so much. "He's in Greenfield, right? That's so close. Maybe he didn't even hear you." Sarah paused. "Hey, what if you show him an old picture of Lottie without saying anything and see what happens? My great-grandpa doesn't always remember who I am, but he still remembers stuff from a long time ago. He knows exactly what happened when he was young. If this man doesn't recognize Lottie, it probably means he's not even the right person."

"I do have a picture I could show him." Charlie hesitated, glancing up at the bulletin board. "Maybe I could try... but maybe it would be better just to talk to him a little first and see what he says when he sees me...?" Her voice trailed off uncertainly.

"I wish I was there. I'd go with you tomorrow," Sarah said.

Charlie groaned and flopped on her bed. "There's no way I can go tomorrow, anyway. We have auditions right before Mom and I leave for Florida."

"You're going to do great, Charlie!" Sarah exclaimed. "You're practically the only one in the orchestra who always pays attention, and you play with heart. You ought to be concertmaster."

"Way wrong, but thanks a lot." Charlie rolled onto her back and stretched her legs in the air. She felt a bit better, somehow. "I really miss you in orchestra this year."

"I miss you, too!" Sarah sighed. "So, has Mr. Fernandez made his Carnegie Hall joke yet? And is cute Devin still driving you crazy?"

"*Cute* Devin?" Charlie blushed.

"C'mon, don't you think he's cute?" Sarah said sternly, but Charlie could tell she was trying hard to cheer her up.

"Yeah, yes—okay! Devin's *kind* of cute—for a cellist, that is..."

The girls dissolved into waves of giggles. Charlie's sides ached, but it felt so good.

CHAPTER FIFTEEN

Audition day. Charlie's hands were trembling. They'd started trembling last night as she finished packing for her trip to Florida, and they'd been shaking all through the morning as she silently practiced finger patterns on her desk in science and math. At 11:10 a.m., her assigned time, Charlie joined the group of kids lined up in front of the auditorium to wait for their auditions. She stood quietly clutching her hands as she stared at the concrete floor. When her turn came, she raised her head, squared her shoulders, and entered the auditorium alone, taking her place in the center of the stage.

Charlie took a deep breath as she lifted her violin, planted her feet, and blinked her eyes. She'd practiced and practiced. She had this! But as soon as she began to play the Mozart concerto, her left hand froze and would hardly budge. She fumbled on the very first measure, already off tempo, unable to place her fingers where they needed to go.

Mr. Fernandez let her start over twice. Then Ms. Patel stopped her for a moment to say: "Is something on your mind, Charlie, dear? Relax and concentrate on the music!"

Relax? Who was she kidding? Every high note sounded flat, and her E string was squeaking like a mouse. How in the world had Lottie played with the symphony in Vienna without making a mistake? No matter how hard Charlie practiced, she could never be that good. If Nana Rose had been there watching her audition, she would have been nothing but disappointed.

The third time Charlie stumbled, Mr. Fernandez rose from his chair. "Do you want to give that one last try?"

"Perhaps a different piece of music?" Ms. Patel suggested.

Charlie shook her head and scrambled for the door.

"We'll post the results on Wednesday morning. Have a nice weekend," Ms. Patel called after her. She leaned toward Mr. Fernandez and whispered something that sounded a lot like "What a shame," as Charlie darted from the room.

Oh...no, no, *no!* Charlie wiped her eyes with a sleeve. Directly in front of her was the blurry image of Devin, standing against the wall in the hallway, waiting for his turn. She'd have to walk straight past him as quickly as possible.

"Hey, Charlie!" Devin pointed his bow at her.

"Something wrong?" Charlie nearly tripped as she picked up speed.

"Turn around, you've got something on your shirt."

 74

Charlie stopped short and felt behind her back. A small piece of rosin was stuck between her shoulder blades. She had *no idea* how it could have gotten there.

"How'd your audition go?" Devin asked as she brushed the rosin off.

Charlie opened her mouth to say, "I blew it! It was *horrible!*" But no words came out—only a strange wheezing noise followed by a sharp squeak that sounded just like her E string.

The hallway and everything in it started to swirl in slow motion. Devin's eyes opened wide, and the two sixth graders standing next to him bent forward, laughing.

It was official, Charlie thought: the most embarrassing day of her life.

Ms. Patel stepped out of the auditorium. With an enthusiastic wave, she motioned for Devin to come in.

Devin hesitated for a minute. He coughed twice and tilted his head toward Charlie, but she had already fled up the hallway.

CHAPTER SIXTEEN

Charlie dropped off her early dismissal slip and sped away on her bike. When she finally got home, at least Mom didn't notice how miserable she looked. Mom was too busy getting ready for their trip to see Nana Rose.

"Are you all set, Charlie? The cab will be here in ten minutes," Mom said without glancing up from her to-do list on the kitchen table.

Jake jogged into the kitchen, dribbling a basketball. He was home early, too, after a dentist appointment.

"Don't forget your homework while we're away this weekend," Mom said as she checked the last items off her list. "And have fun with Dad." She reached up to give Jake a hug.

"No worries. I hardly have any homework—and guess what? Dad and I are going out for barbecue tonight." Jake turned to Charlie and smacked his lips. "Chicken and ribs—dee-licious!"

Charlie was about to grab the basketball from him and kick it into the family room when Jake took her by the elbow and pulled her aside. "You okay? You seem kind of...sad."

"I just had my orchestra audition," Charlie said in a low voice. "It's no big deal."

"Don't worry. I'm sure you rocked it." Jake dribbled the ball between his legs.

Charlie shook her head and shrugged. "We'll see. Please don't say anything to Mom, okay? I mean, she and Dad obviously know about my audition, but I didn't exactly tell them that it was this morning."

"Totally get it." Jake grinned. "You didn't want Mom doing the worried-Mom routine and throwing off your game, right?" He held the basketball still for a minute. "Seriously, though, Charlie, cheer up—you'll be fine. And you're going to Florida this weekend; that'll be cool."

"Yeah..."

Jake gave her arm a gentle tug. "Hey, text me if you find out anything interesting from Nana. You know...about Lottie."

"Okay," Charlie said, feeling a little brighter. Jake had never asked her to text him before—or said anything encouraging about her music or anything else, for that matter. When she was little, Charlie used to follow Jake around the house, and he would nearly always chase her away. As they got older, sometimes they'd fight and sometimes they'd call a truce. But they'd never, ever been close like Nana Rose and Lottie.

It would be kind of nice, Charlie thought, if she and Jake could maybe hang out sometimes.

Nana Rose was pacing anxiously as she waited in the lobby at Clover Manor. She wore pink fuzzy slippers and a hand-knit cardigan. Charlie hadn't seen her since she'd moved to Florida in June and suddenly realized just how much she'd missed her.

The worried look on Nana Rose's face turned to joy as she caught sight of her daughter and granddaughter. Charlie sprinted ahead to her open arms.

"Schnuckelpuss! How happy I am to see you!"

"How are you feeling, Mama?" Mom asked loudly.

"I'm fine, always fine, nothing to complain about." Nana Rose smiled and kissed them both twice. "Life is easier here. I like seeing the sun shine every day, and I won't miss the snow this winter!"

Charlie glanced around the lobby. Clover Manor was nothing like Nana Rose's old house in Connecticut, with its wide plank floors and large, cluttered kitchen that always smelled like warm apples. The towering entryway was two stories high and had pink marble floors and gray stone columns. One entire wall was made of mirrors. It was hot enough outside for Charlie to be wearing shorts, but now, standing inside, she felt an icy chill. The lobby air even smelled cold; it stung her nostrils.

"Let me show you my room, and we can chat a little before

78

dinner," Nana Rose said. "I wish I could have baked you some nice brownies, but there's no kitchen; we have every meal in the big dining room." She sighed.

"That's okay, Nana." Charlie took her grandmother's arm. "I had way too many cookies on the plane, and I'm still pretty full."

Nana Rose led them down a green tiled corridor to a tidy room with a mauve couch and a small coffee table covered with a lace cloth. The shelves behind the couch were filled with art books, floral teacups, and photographs. There was a framed picture of Grandpa Sam at the beach with Jake when he was little. Another photo showed a much taller Jake with his basketball team, carrying a trophy. Charlie smiled to see a picture of herself at five or six holding a quarter-sized violin, with an excited grin; two of her bottom teeth were missing.

"Come here beside me, Charlie, and tell me about your music." Nana Rose patted the overstuffed sofa cushions. "Sit close so I can catch every word. Are you practicing each day?"

"I try to," Charlie said, "most days, anyway."

"She practices all the time!" Mom chuckled. "I can hear her from my office."

"You must be playing more difficult pieces this year, am I right? Music that stretches the intellect as well as the fingers." Nana lightly tapped her forehead. "Interpreting what the composer wishes to convey, the story behind the music—that's what makes a great musician."

"I guess so," Charlie said cautiously. "But the thing is, I still make a few mistakes when I play. Lots of them, actually." She stared down at the lace cloth on the table.

"Why, that means nothing!" Nana Rose shook her head and smiled. "All the finest musicians hit a sour note from time to time. When you challenge yourself, when you take risks— it's to be expected. The important thing, my darling, is that you feel the music inside you, that it becomes part of your inner spirit." Leaning closer, Nana Rose looked straight into Charlie's eyes. "No musician is born confident! Confidence must be earned. If you love music, what counts—the only thing that truly matters—is that you try."

"I miss you so much, Nana," Charlie whispered. How was it that Nana Rose always managed to make her feel better, without even knowing it?

Nana Rose took both Charlie's hands in her own and squeezed them tight. "Now then, I have been considering all that I must tell you . . . I mean, for your research about Lottie." Nana Rose briefly closed her eyes when she said her sister's name. "I've put aside a few things." She rubbed one hand along her temple. "I took them out this morning; where could they be?"

"Can I help?" Mom asked.

"I'll be fine. You relax and be comfortable; I won't be a minute." Nana Rose disappeared through an arched doorway and returned a few moments later carrying a leather book. The tattered cover was decorated with delicate flowers and inscribed at the top with an elaborate R.

"What's that, Nana?"

"Something special. I have here my own scrapbook. I brought it with me when I was a child from Vienna."

"For heaven's sakes!" Mom exclaimed. "I don't recall ever seeing that before." Charlie was surprised by the strain in Mom's voice. Mom, who was always so calm, so matter-of-fact and practical, sounded confused and almost a little hurt.

"To be honest with you, darling, I forgot about it, too," Nana Rose replied without looking up. "I found this in the attic when we packed up the old house in Connecticut, before I moved to Florida."

Charlie saw a strange expression cross Nana Rose's face, the kind of expression that made her wonder whether she was telling the whole truth.

Nana Rose placed the scrapbook on the coffee table and opened it up to the first page.

"Oh, Nana, that picture is beautiful!" Charlie exclaimed. The page was filled with a pastel drawing of a princess with flowing blond hair. In her lap sat a plump mouse wearing a tiara.

"My cousin Trudy drew pictures for me when I was a little girl." Nana Rose smoothed her trim gray curls. "I had long hair, like you do, and it was as blond as flax—oh yes, it's true! How I loved the fairy stories. Trudy was an artist; she could draw almost anything."

"What happened to Cousin Trudy?" Charlie started to ask, but stopped when she saw a dark look in her grandmother's eyes. Trudy had obviously not been one of the lucky ones.

"Let me find what I wanted to show you." Nana Rose searched through pages filled with black-and-white photographs and colorful drawings.

"Wait, is that you?" Mom pointed to the sepia photo of a blond baby sitting in a young girl's lap. The baby's round face was creased with dimples, and the girl had dark curls cascading below her waist.

"Yes, it's me—I was a chubby baby, wasn't I?" Nana Rose smiled at Charlie.

"And that must be Lottie holding you," Charlie said.

"Of course—she was only eight or nine in that picture, but look how she is already so lovely. Such glorious curls!" Nana Rose flipped the page. "Ah, this is what I wanted you to see."

Charlie caught her breath. A piece of faded newsprint, spotted brown at the edges, had been glued onto the center of the page. It was the photo of Lottie with her violin, the same photo that was pinned to Charlie's bulletin board at home. "Lottie was in the newspaper?"

"Many times," Nana Rose replied. "This is a review of her concert with the Vienna Philharmonic. Underneath her picture, it says *Wunderkind*. The critic speaks of her extraordinary technique, but even more, how she plays with such intense feeling, straight from the heart. This was Lottie's true gift."

"What music was it?" Charlie stared at the newsprint to see if she could tell.

"Let me see. Here it is: Violin Concerto No. 3 in G Major by Mozart."

"Violin Concerto No. 3 in G Major?" Charlie gasped. "That's what Lottie played onstage?"

"You don't care for Mozart?" Nana Rose asked.

"I love Mozart! That's one of my favorite pieces! I played a section of it for my audition this morning."

"Your audition?" Mom's head jerked up. "What? You already *had* your audition? But Charlie, you didn't mention it to me."

Charlie exhaled. "Oops." Then she whispered, "Can we talk about it later, please?" She turned to Nana Rose. "Were there other reviews like this one?"

"Oh yes! Dear Lottie was well known in music circles. She would have become a celebrated soloist, if only..." Nana Rose stopped midsentence and rubbed her knees with the back of her hands. "Well"—she took a deep breath and continued—"I have something else for you, darling—a surprise." She started to close the scrapbook.

"Wait a minute," Charlie said, "this one is in English."

Pasted onto the very last page was a small newspaper clipping from the classified section of the *New York Times*. The date was May 12, 1955.

"You can go ahead and read it," Nana Rose said quietly.

Charlie took the scrapbook into her lap. Bits of dust and newsprint crumbled onto her legs. Her throat began to tighten. "Nana?"

"Go ahead."

With a deep breath, Charlie read aloud: "Searching for

Lottie: Beloved Charlotte Kulka. Born 1922 in Vienna, last seen in Budapest, Hungary, 1940. Dark curly hair and blue eyes. Greatly loved and missed." Charlie lowered the book. Nana Rose sat silently, staring up at the ceiling. A single tear slid down the side of her wrinkled cheek.

"Oh, Nana," Charlie said.

Nana Rose wiped the tear away. With a sad nod, she took Charlie's hand. "After the war ended, we wrote countless letters—to Herr Hinkleman in Budapest, to the Red Cross—anyone we could think of. My poor mother was desperate. She wanted to travel to Hungary to search for my sister, but we were alone; we had no money, it was impossible."

"You didn't hear back?" Charlie asked.

"Some of our letters were returned, but there were no answers."

"Oh!" Charlie's lips were suddenly quivering.

"But still we tried." Nana Rose looked straight into Charlie's eyes. "We never gave up hope. What have I always said? Miracles can happen!" She dabbed her eyes and smiled at her granddaughter. Mom's eyes were damp now, too.

"I have something to tell you, Nana, something really important," Charlie said in a rush. "I might have found your cousin Nathan, the one in Lottie's music journal."

"What?" Mom exclaimed. "What do you mean?"

"You think you found Nathan?" Nana Rose's eyes opened wide. "How could that be?"

"What exactly is going on?" Mom demanded.

"I found Nathan Kulka's name in Lottie's journal—remember, I showed it to you, Mom? Nana told me he was a dentist, and that she thought she saw his name on a sign in Bridgeport a long time ago. So I checked the phone listings, just in case, and I found somebody with that name." Charlie stopped to catch her breath. "It turns out that he lives near us, at the Connecticut Helping Home for Seniors in Greenfield. I tried calling there last week."

"You're kidding!" Mom gasped.

Charlie covered her eyes with her hands. "I think I might have even spoken to him."

"My darling Charlie!" Nana Rose exclaimed. "How fantastic and astonishing!"

"Why didn't you tell me?" Mom shook her head. "You didn't breathe a word!"

"I'm sorry." Charlie shrugged. "I wasn't trying to keep it a secret. I'm just not exactly sure that it's him, because—"

"What did he say to you?" Nana Rose asked eagerly.

"Nothing, really." Charlie paused for a moment and wondered whether to tell the truth: that this man who might be Cousin Nathan was certain that Lottie was dead. Nana Rose's eyes were gleaming. "Honestly, though," Charlie continued, "he seemed pretty mixed up. I don't know if he really understood what I was asking. It might not be him at all."

"Dear Nathan," Nana Rose said softly. "Wouldn't it be remarkable if he was living in Connecticut this whole time! It would make sense...the Jewish Agency found jobs for refugees in many places, including cities and towns in Connecticut. There was a great need for people in the medical field. If Nathan became a dentist, he might have been placed in Bridgeport." She sighed. "Schnuckelpuss, you must go visit him."

"But Nana, he might not even be the right guy."

"Listen to me, darling." Nana Rose patted Charlie's hand. "Maybe this fellow is Cousin Nathan, and wouldn't that be something! Or maybe he's just a lonely man who could use a little sunshine. Bring your violin with you."

"My violin?"

"Yes. I have it on good authority that old people love music." Nana Rose smiled. "You must go there as soon as possible. If it's Nathan—you will give him a big hug for me, won't you? Stranger things have happened. Some families were reunited years after the war."

"Don't worry, Mama. I'll take Charlie there next weekend to check out this Nathan Kulka, I assure you." Out of the corner of her eye, Charlie could see Mom shaking her head as she looked first at her mother, then at her daughter.

"Now, Charlie..." Nana Rose put one hand into the pocket of her cardigan. "I have something I've been saving for you ever since you were born. It belonged to my sister. I intended to wait until your bat mitzvah, but I think you'll appreciate it more right now." She pulled out a black velvet box. "Open it."

Charlie held the box in the palms of her hands. It took a moment to figure out how to unlock the tiny brass latch.

When she opened the lid, she blinked twice. At the bottom of the box lay a gold necklace with a small pendant in the shape of a Mogen David—a Star of David. "Did this really belong to...?"

"Yes, it was Lottie's. It is solid gold—a 'serious piece,' as dear Mutti would say. My parents didn't allow Lottie to take it with her when she went to study music in Budapest, and so I have the necklace for you still. It's for you, Charlie, her name-sake, since you are practically a young woman now."

Charlie closed the box and hugged her grandmother tight. "Oh, Nana, it's so pretty! I'll wear it for my bat mitzvah next spring."

On the flight home from Florida, Charlie gazed over the clouds. The rest of the weekend with Nana Rose had been great. They'd met some of Nana's neighbors and taken her shopping at a nearby mall. Charlie and Mom had even spent an hour on Saturday floating in Clover Manor's pool and playing shuffleboard while Nana rested. Then they'd all gone out for dinner and a movie.

But now, all Charlie could think about was Nana Rose and her sister Lottie's lives before the war. Nana had described her sister as "fearless." Lottie was brave enough to perform in a concert with adults and brave enough to leave her family to go study music in Budapest. But was she strong enough to have survived the Holocaust? Charlie shuddered.

"Are you all right?" Mom put down her newspaper.

"It's just that…" Charlie shook her head. "I just don't understand why Nana Rose didn't try harder to find Cousin Nathan. And why didn't she ever show you all those photographs and Lottie's concert reviews? You said you'd never seen her scrapbook before."

Mom sighed and stretched her arm around Charlie's shoulder. "I know it's hard to understand. To be honest, when I was your age, it wasn't easy for me, either. I was an only child, and my parents doted on me; our small family couldn't have been closer. But there were things I knew I couldn't—shouldn't—ask them." Mom stopped and exhaled slowly, realizing that she hadn't explained much at all. "Let me put it this way: Imagine if you were Nana Rose and you had lost…well, everything, and you had to start over. You wouldn't want to always be reminded of the old life that was gone forever, would you?"

"But Nana's dad was killed by the Nazis! And she lost her sister, too. Why wouldn't she want to look at their pictures? Why would she put them away?" Charlie frowned.

Mom looked into Charlie's eyes. "You know how Nana is always so upbeat and cheerful, even when things go wrong?"

Charlie nodded. "Nana *never* gets mad." She remembered the time Nana Rose had been babysitting and Jake had decided to make popcorn. He'd left the pan on the stove while he went outside to play basketball. Within minutes, the smoke alarm went off. It was connected to the alarm system, and before Nana could figure out how to turn it off, the fire department had arrived at the door. Instead of scolding Jake, Nana Rose had greeted the firefighters with apricot rugelach and taken Charlie and Jake outside to admire the fire truck.

"After I had children of my own," Mom said softly, "I realized—or I least, I understood a bit better—that my mother had to bury the sad parts of her life in order to live happily."

"So Nana tried to forget about everything?" Charlie asked.

"No, not exactly, but she needed to look ahead and, especially, make sure that our lives were full of happiness and not overshadowed by such deep sadness. That was her private way to defeat the Nazis."

"You mean Nana didn't want to mess you up."

"Yes." Mom nodded. "Something like that."

Charlie dug her nails into her palms. She'd thought Lottie was the strong one, but suddenly she realized that it was Nana Rose who'd had to be fearless.

"And . . . what about now?" Charlie searched Mom's face.

"Now Nana is an old woman, as are all the survivors. I can see how glad she is to share her stories with you; keeping the family memories alive means the world to her."

"Mom . . ." It was suddenly hard for Charlie to speak. "Sometimes I wonder if I have to—that maybe I need to be who Lottie couldn't be. For Nana." She hesitated, remembering Dad's assurances that Nana was already proud of her. But was that enough? Charlie took a deep breath. "I don't ever want to let Nana down. She thinks that someday I can, you know, be as good as Lottie was—amazing on the violin."

There. She had said it.

Mom looked at her for a long moment, then reached for her hand. "Tell me the truth, Charlie. Do you enjoy playing in the orchestra? I mean, is there something else you'd rather try?"

"I love the violin!" Charlie replied without hesitation. "I love it more than anything! It's just that I'm not...I'm not totally sure I want to be a soloist like Lottie. Or that I even could ever be good enough." Charlie's voice picked up speed. "But what if—what if I was thinking about something else? Like...maybe becoming a music teacher, like Mr. Fernandez? It could be really cool to teach kids about music! But if I wanted to do that instead...do you think Nana Rose would mind? I mean, wouldn't she be disappointed?"

Mom brought her face so close to Charlie's that their noses were almost touching. "Nana Rose's greatest joy is to watch you grow into the wonderful young woman you were meant to be. I think you would make a *fantastic* music teacher someday, sweetheart—but whatever you decide, decide for yourself. *Be* yourself! That's the best way to remember Lottie. It's more than enough, I promise."

As soon as they got home Sunday evening, Charlie ran up to her room and locked the door. She pulled the velvet box from her purse and carefully took out the gold necklace. The chain was long and woven in intricate links. Charlie fastened the chain at the back of her neck. The Star of David pendant felt smooth and cool. When she flipped it over, she noticed a faint inscription etched on the back: JS.

JS. Wait—she *knew* those initials!

Charlie quickly texted Sarah: **Nana gave me Lottie's gold necklace with a Star of David. It says JS on the back! Must be Johann Schmidt, the boy from her music journal, right?**

Sarah's reply took two seconds. **Yes!**

Charlie ran her fingers over the beautiful necklace. She still didn't know what to make of her conversation with the man who *might* be Nana's cousin, Nathan Kulka, and what he'd claimed about Lottie's fate. But could the initials on the Star of David be some sort of sign?

Charlie spun around and grinned at the photo on the bulletin board. Lottie was patiently smiling back.

CHAPTER SEVENTEEN

Early Wednesday morning, Charlie lay in bed with the duvet pulled over her face. It seemed like she'd barely gone to sleep when her alarm started buzzing. Audition results would be posted in front of the auditorium today for everyone to see. There was no way she'd make concertmaster after her miserable audition. She'd probably spend another year in the middle of the first section, if she was lucky, or even drop into the second section next to Garrett Goodness, the quiet and polite boy who was tone-deaf and held his bow in a knot with his fist. Charlie tugged the covers higher until her toes were sticking out. Suddenly, her face was burning hot. Thank goodness! Maybe she had a fever and would have to spend the whole day in bed.

Mom called from the bottom of the stairs, "Past time to get up! You don't want to be late."

"I might be sick!" Charlie yelled into the quilt. She kicked the covers onto the floor. She had to go to school. There was no use putting it off.

When Charlie left the house, Mom came to wave goodbye at the door, just like when Charlie and Jake were little. "*Hals und Beinbruch,* darling."

"Doesn't that mean 'Break a leg' in German?" Charlie asked.

"Something along those lines," Mom replied, smiling.

Charlie rolled her eyes. "How is it supposed to be lucky?"

"Well, Nana Rose always used to say that to me when I was your age, and it did bring me luck!" Mom wrapped a light scarf around Charlie's neck. "It was a special weekend with Nana, wasn't it?"

Charlie nodded. "I'm sorry I didn't tell you about my audition, Mom—I mean, before we saw Nana Rose. I was just nervous."

Mom kissed Charlie's forehead. "Call me from school as soon as you find out whether you made concertmaster."

Normally the bus ride was bumpy and boring, but today Charlie wished it would last forever. When she got to school, there were already a few kids standing in front of the music department notice board.

Charlie held her breath and began counting backward. "Ten, nine, eight, seven, six..." At three, she forced herself to look up. Her jaw clenched. Concertmaster: Tommy Lee.

She felt sick. A ripple of nausea hit her stomach as she

scanned the rest of the list. Where was her name? Could they have kicked her out of the orchestra entirely? Gazing down the list for the first section, there it was: fourth chair, only slightly better than last year. Two eighth graders who were solid, but hardly standout players, were seated ahead of her. Charlie felt foolish that she'd imagined she had any real talent, when Lottie had been extraordinary enough to play solo with the symphony in Vienna.

"Hey, Charlie, where'd they put you?"

Oh no, not again! Charlie glanced sideways at the cello list. First chair for Devin, of course. No surprises there.

"So where's your seat?" Devin repeated, tossing his hair out of his eyes. Devin's hair was so long that Charlie wondered how he could see his sheet music.

"Nowhere special," Charlie muttered. What a stupid thing to say!

"You played Mozart for your audition, right?"

"More like *No-start,*" Charlie whispered under her breath. Did Devin's eyelashes actually touch his nose?

"So... are you going to try out for the school musical?" Devin turned as if he was talking to someone else, but there wasn't anyone else around.

"I can't sing," Charlie replied. "I'm horrible at singing." *And violin,* she added silently.

"I meant the pit orchestra," Devin said, leaning against the notice board. "There's an audition, but I've heard they basically take everyone."

"Oh." Charlie shrugged. "I haven't thought about it."

"Well, you should." Devin looked down at his toes. "You rock on the violin."

Charlie wondered if he was teasing her.

"Playing in the pit is cool," Devin added. "They let you out of class to practice."

"Well, yeah...maybe." Charlie looked down to check her toes, too. "If it's okay with my mom..." Oh no—did she really just say that?

"I know, my mom hates driving me everywhere. Maybe we could carpool to practices," Devin replied.

Carpool? Did Devin actually ask her to carpool?

"Oh, bummer!" Devin glanced at his phone. "We're late for homeroom."

"Yeah, *bummer!*" Charlie replied with a dizzy grin.

She texted the news to Sarah, and a reassuring buzz came right back: **Could be worse. They ALWAYS pick eighth graders to lead violins. You'll be concertmaster next year!**

Charlie sighed. Then she laughed as another message came in.

Also, Tommy Lee is kinda CUTE. Just like Devin!

Sarah had a point. Maybe she would try out for the musical, Charlie decided, just in case it was fun.

CHAPTER EIGHTEEN

When Charlie got home from school, Mom was crouched by the front door, vigorously dusting the shoe storage bench. It looked as if she had been dusting for a while.

"How'd it go? I've been waiting to hear—" Mom stopped when she saw the answer in Charlie's stony expression. "Honey, I'm terribly sorry."

"It's no big deal; I didn't think I was going to make concertmaster anyway," Charlie quickly replied.

Mom stood and gave Charlie a hug. "There's always next year—if that's what you really want," she said. Then she handed Charlie an envelope. "This arrived for you."

Charlie ran up the steps to her room. When she opened the envelope, a short note and a photograph fell into her lap.

Charlie dearest,

I am still thinking with such happiness about your visit! Just

after you left, I found this photo. I believe you will recognize Lottie,
but if I am right, the young man beside her is none other than Cousin
Nathan Kulka. I cannot be one hundred percent certain, of course—I
last saw Nathan when I was only a youngster. You must tell me what
you find when you see him!

I love you, and I know that you are a brave and wonderful girl.

xoxo,

Nana Rose

PS—I must correct myself, Schnuckelpuss. I think you are a
brave and lovely young woman!

Charlie stared at the old photo. It was ripped at the edges
so that the legs and feet of the two people in it were missing.
The teenage girl was definitely Lottie. She looked especially
grown-up in a black dress and long white gloves. Her hair
was tucked under a velvet cap with a feather on one side. Lottie gazed straight into the camera with wide eyes and a broad
smile. Her mouth was slightly open as if she was about to speak.

Standing next to Lottie, his elbow just touching hers, was
a young man in a double-breasted jacket. He had short dark
hair parted in the middle and large ears that stuck out from his
head. Charlie noticed that the boy's arms extended the same
way as his ears; they were longer than his jacket.

Charlie pinned the photo on her bulletin board next to the
picture of Lottie with her violin. Was the boy Nathan Kulka?
And was it really possible that this same Nathan Kulka was
alive and living at the seniors' home in Greenfield?

There was less than two weeks left before the family history report was due. Charlie sighed and opened her computer; she still needed to look at the Holocaust Memorial Museum website. Eerie black-and-white photographs popped up that reminded her of the ones in her own family's album.

As Charlie clicked through the photos, her stomach tightened. Who were all these people? These men and women captured in their old-fashioned clothing with their families and their friends; the ones who had disappeared like the billowing clouds outside her window? Children in rags appeared, wearing Jewish stars on thin coats, and finally, children with haunted, hollowed eyes wearing prison uniforms.

Once, Charlie had tried to get Mom to go through their family photos from Europe but was disappointed to find that Mom could only identify a few of the faces. When Charlie asked how many of the people in the photo album had survived the Holocaust, Mom simply looked away.

"Who did you celebrate holidays with?" Charlie had asked. "If it was just Nana Rose and her mother who came to America, and you were an only child, where did you go for Passover and Hanukkah?"

"Well…" Mom thought for a minute. "We had cousins on my father's side. Your grandfather Sam's parents emigrated from Russia in the 1920s. And Nana had many close friends among the refugee community. My 'aunts and uncles' growing up were mostly dear friends who had lost their loved ones, too. They were always there for each other, nearly like family."

Then Mom told Charlie how her mother's friends had helped bake pastries for her wedding. Mom smiled as she recalled how all the guests had been delighted by the expansive display of Viennese and Hungarian desserts. The wedding cake had been a spectacular seven-layer Dobos torte.

Charlie heard a rustling noise and glanced out her bedroom window. The branches of a tall oak scraped against the panes of glass. When Charlie was little, she used to stare at that tree, wondering whether she could reach out and climb onto its branches. Would it be possible, she wondered, would she ever dare to swing over its limbs and scramble down to the safety of the ground below?

The sound of an enormous burp made her jump.

"Nervous or something?" Jake was standing at her door, smirking.

"That's disgusting! How can you be so gross?"

"Naturally talented, perhaps?" Jake laughed.

"Ha! Looks to me like you've been practicing."

"Yeah, well, you've got your violin, and I've got my own talents to nurture." Jake ambled through the door and sank down on Charlie's rug. "So, I heard Mom and Dad talking about this dude—the cousin guy you seem to have found at the seniors' home..."

"You mean Nathan Kulka?"

"Yup, him." Jake cocked his head sideways. "Do you think he could actually be *related* to us?"

"I'm not really sure," Charlie said, "but maybe."

"Well, it was pretty solid of you to find him. I gotta give you kudos for that one."

Charlie swallowed air and coughed. A compliment... from Jake?

"Thanks," she replied as if nothing special had happened.

Jake leaned over Charlie's shoulder. "I mean, even if you can't find Nana's sister, it would be pretty intense if you found us a cousin we didn't know existed."

"You think?" That was two compliments from Jake. Charlie tried not to let him see her smile, but she didn't have to worry because he was looking at something poking out from under the bed.

"What's that?"

"Oh." Charlie blushed. "It's just an old-fashioned toy I found in the basement a couple of weeks ago. Nana gave it to me when I was little."

"Oh yeah, I remember that thing! It's your diabolo." Jake pulled the large rubber top with its two short wands from beneath Charlie's bed. He tried balancing the top on the string tied between the wands. With a long swoop, he tossed it into the air, but the toy hit the ceiling with a thwack and came crashing down, narrowly missing the lamp.

"I guess I'm still lousy at this!" Jake laughed. "You try."

Charlie took the top and rested it on the string. It felt awkward and uneven, and then suddenly, her wrists moved and the top was spinning. Without even remembering how, her hands seemed to know the way to make the wands push and pull while the top spun faster and faster.

"Not bad!" Jake whistled.

Charlie glanced at the ceiling, then tossed the diabolo so that it spun in the air—just shy of the hanging light—and returned to the string, still in motion.

"Wow. You're really good."

Charlie blushed. "Hey, Jake?"

"Yeah?"

"You know how Nana Rose always says there are miracles in the world?"

"Oh, sure," Jake snorted, "and how about, 'If at first you don't succeed...'"

"'...try, try again!'" Charlie said. "But seriously, do you think Nana's right? Do you think there can ever be *real* miracles?"

Jake licked his lips and rubbed his chin. "Well, let's put it this way—you remember that girl I met on vacation last summer?"

"You mean the supermodel-hot-way-out-of-your-league girl with the streaky blond hair that I saw you kiss on the ride at Disney World?"

"Yup, she's the one!" Jake was grinning from ear to ear.

"Okay, what's your point?" Charlie asked.

"Well, *that* was a miracle!"

Charlie picked her pillow off the bed and threw it at Jake, this time hitting him squarely on the back of his neck as he scooted out the door.

"Finally!" Charlie raised both hands in the air.

CHAPTER NINETEEN

Saturday came quickly, almost too quickly. Mom had agreed to take Charlie to the seniors' home to look for Nathan Kulka, but she appeared nearly as nervous as Charlie felt as they got into the car.

"Nana Rose told me to bring my violin." Charlie held up the case.

"I remember; that's a good idea. It'll pass the time, in any event, if it turns out..."

"...That the man I talked to isn't our cousin?"

Mom shrugged. "Honestly, honey, we shouldn't get our hopes up too high; we'll have to wait and see." She pulled the keys from her handbag and glanced at the sky. "It looks like rain; you were smart to wear a hat."

Charlie twirled her hair into a bun and pushed a stray curl beneath her cap.

The Connecticut Helping Home for Seniors was a short brick building surrounded by a parking lot overlooking the highway. A rusted link fence encircled the asphalt. There were no trees or grass.

"Do you think this is it?" Mom asked as she parked next to a pair of abandoned hubcaps.

"It looks like a bus station." Charlie looked around cautiously.

Charlie could barely keep up as Mom got out of the car and barreled through the entrance to the reception desk. The hallway walls were white and bare; there wasn't any marble tile or soft mauve couches like the ones at Clover Manor where Nana Rose lived.

A sign stuck on a metal post blocked their way: ALL VISITORS MUST BE ANNOUNCED.

"Hello there!" Mom said in a cheery voice to the young woman sitting behind the desk.

The receptionist peered at them through shaded glasses. She was wearing orange button earrings, and her blond hair was poufed on top of her head. "Can I help you?"

"We're here to see Dr. Nathan Kulka." Mom's voice sounded uncomfortably loud, Charlie thought.

"Oh, that's good. Dr. Kulka doesn't get too many visitors. Hardly any." The woman picked up the phone on her desk. "He is expecting you, right?"

"Well..." Mom hesitated. "Not exactly."

"What'd you say?" The receptionist leaned forward,

keeping one hand on top of the phone. "Who should I tell him is here?" She cocked her head to the side so that her hair looked crooked. "You must be family members, aren't you?"

"Actually, it's kind of a long story," Mom explained. "We *think* Dr. Kulka might be related to us."

"Sort of," added Charlie. *Probably not helpful,* she realized immediately.

The receptionist sat up straight and adjusted her glasses. "I don't understand. I'll need to let him know who's here—it's our policy. Your names, please?"

"The thing is..." Mom began, but Charlie could already tell this wasn't going to work. Then Mom put her hands up. "Roth—My name is Marion Roth."

The receptionist watched them as she dialed the number. "Hello, Dr. Kulka, we've got some visitors for you. Dr. Kulka?" She raised her voice. "It's a Mrs. Roth with her daughter. That's right, Roth. *R-O-T-H.*"

Charlie could see her mother wince.

The receptionist put down the receiver. "I'm sorry, but he says he doesn't want to be disturbed. He might have been sleeping."

"We really do need to meet him," Mom insisted. "He *could* be our long-lost cousin—"

The receptionist stood up, expressionless. "I'm sure you understand that you can't go in if he doesn't want to see you. Maybe you'd better call first next time."

"But I just explained to you, we might be family!" Mom leaned forward. "Is there somebody else I can speak to?"

"There's only me today," the receptionist replied coldly. "And like I already told you, I can't let you in. Sorry." She hurriedly shuffled some papers, placed a small sign on the counter that read BACK IN FIVE MINUTES, and walked into the adjoining office. She pushed the door shut.

"Excuse me!" Mom exclaimed in the direction of the closed door. "Have a heart!" Charlie could see the veins in Mom's neck popping out. "That receptionist is simply...infuriating."

"Mom, she's just doing her job. We'd better go." Charlie yanked on her mother's sleeve.

"Honey, we're here right now. And what if he actually is our cousin, and he's alone and old..." Mom's voice cracked.

"But we can't do anything." Charlie shook her head.

They turned and started back toward the front door. Halfway down the corridor, Charlie spotted a hallway that veered off to the left.

"Look over there!" Charlie exclaimed.

"What is it?" Mom asked.

"Give me a sec, okay?" Charlie lifted her violin case and darted down the hallway. Mom glanced behind them, squeezed her handbag under her arm, and skidded after her.

At the opening at the end of the hall, five or six people were sitting in metal armchairs, watching a small TV. Charlie searched from face to face. They were all elderly women;

a few held knitting needles or newspapers. One of the women smiled but said nothing.

"I'm sorry, Mom," Charlie whispered. "I thought I saw him!"

"You mean Nathan Kulka? But Charlie—how would you even know?"

Suddenly a shadow crept into the corner of Charlie's eyes. An old man wearing a long blue bathrobe was just beyond the next doorway, shuffling down the hall with a cane.

"Mom, come on..."

"Charlie, stop right now. What is going on?"

"Look at his ears!" Charlie exclaimed. "They stick straight out."

"For heaven's sakes, that's rude," Mom responded.

"They stand way out," Charlie repeated under her breath.

The old man stood still for a moment, holding on to the doorframe.

"We should leave." Mom put her hand on Charlie's arm. "We have no idea who that man is."

Charlie pulled away and leapt forward: "Dr. Kulka?"

The old man turned to see who was calling. Suddenly, his mouth dropped open. *"Mein liebchen!"* He raised one hand and clutched his chest. "Is it you? I thought...I was certain you were dead!"

"What?" Charlie froze.

"You've come back to Budapest; I prayed you would come! And you've brought your instrument. Yes, for the concert!" Tears sprang into the corners of his wrinkled eyes.

"It's my violin," Charlie said hoarsely.

"I think there's some mistake." Mom's face was ashen. "This is my daughter, Charlie; we've never met before."

"Haven't you come back for good?" The old man shook his head. "I waited for such a long while."

Charlie felt so hot she could hardly breathe. She pulled off her cap, and red curls tumbled over her shoulders.

The old man sprang backward, clutching his cane. "Who are you?"

"I'm Charlie Roth—we spoke on the phone, do you remember? Mom and I came to see you because, well, we might be relatives."

"No! I don't know you! No! No! No!" The old man closed his eyes. "I don't know. There are so many things I forget these days," he added wearily.

Mom reached forward, gently touching his arm. "Let me explain. We are looking for Dr. Nathan Kulka. We think we might be related. We'd like to talk about the old days, about our family..."

The man's eyes opened wide. Ignoring Mom, he searched Charlie's face. "Did Johann send you?"

"Johann? Do you mean Johann Schmidt?" Charlie gasped. Maybe she hadn't heard him correctly. "Do you know Johann?"

The old man ran a finger along his lips thoughtfully. He rocked back and forth, staring into space as if trying to recall. "We must save as many as possible," he finally said. "Get them to the hills to safety."

"Please," Mom tried again. "Can we sit with you for a moment?"

A loud voice thundered across the hallway. "Hey, lady, what're you doin' in there?" A tall, square security guard appeared. The receptionist stood behind him, pointing her finger.

"We're just visiting, that's all," Mom said.

"They snuck right by me." The receptionist stared at Charlie.

"Do you know these people, sir?" the guard asked in a stern voice.

"Never seen 'em before. Perfect strangers!" The old man rubbed his nose with his wrist.

"Lady, you gotta come with me." The guard motioned with a sharp jab of his finger.

"But we have to talk to Dr. Kulka," Mom said. "If you'll just—"

"I want you and your daughter out of here immediately!" The guard pointed in the direction of the front door.

Mom turned toward the old man. "Here is our address and phone number." She pulled out a business card and dropped it into the pocket of his bathrobe. "We may be cousins. Lottie Kulka was my aunt, and Rose Kulka is my mother."

The old man shook his head sadly. "I don't know those people. Never seen 'em before."

"*Now, lady!*" The guard stepped forward.

"We'll return soon to visit you." Mom squeezed the old

man's hand, then wrapped an arm around Charlie's shoulders. "Okay, I guess we'd better go."

Charlie took one last look. The long wrinkled face was nothing like the boy in the photograph. Only the large ears were the same. "When we come back, I'll play my violin for you."

He nodded, his head shaking ever so slightly, silent.

On the way home, Charlie stared out the window, her head resting against the seat.

"We can try again." Mom broke the silence.

"It won't make any difference." Charlie pressed her nose against the glass. "It's too late. He won't remember anything. He seemed to sort of remember, but then he couldn't. He's just too old and confused."

"We'll find a way." Mom's head bobbed up and down. "Remember what Nana Rose always says: 'If at first you don't succeed...'"

"'...Try, try again.' I know, Mom, but honestly, it's kind of lame. We're never going to find out what happened to Lottie." Charlie's throat felt so thick it was hard to talk.

"Oh, honey, I don't know what to say." Mom sighed. "I suppose I got my hopes up for a minute, too."

"Can we at least go back and bring him something good to eat?" Charlie turned toward her mother. "I bet the food there is terrible. We could make him some cookies, or even ask Nana Rose for her strudel recipe."

"Absolutely! We'll do that."

A truck wheezed by them on the highway. Charlie's stomach tightened. "What are we going to tell Nana?"

"We'll tell her that we met a very sweet gentleman from Budapest and that we plan to visit him again soon." Mom's voice was firm.

"I didn't even get a chance to play my violin." Charlie sighed.

"You'll do it next time, sweetheart. I promise. I'm sure that...I know that *Cousin Nathan* would love to hear you play."

CHAPTER TWENTY

There was no avoiding orchestra rehearsal on Monday morning. Charlie couldn't think of a single excuse for skipping. Now that seats were officially assigned, everyone would see that she wasn't the best violinist after all. She kept her head low as she walked into the rehearsal room and watched Tommy take his place as concertmaster. Tommy raised his violin and deftly warmed up with a few measures from Brandenburg Concerto No. 3 in G Major. The high school chamber ensemble had played the same music at their spring concert, Charlie realized.

"What's up?" Devin was heading toward her.

Charlie was about to say "Hey" in return when she realized that Devin was talking to Tommy. She quickly closed her mouth and opened her violin case, but before she had a chance to sit down, Mr. Fernandez clapped his hands. "Good morning, everyone! Hope you all had a terrific weekend."

Why was Mr. Fernandez being so cheerful?

"I know you've seen your new seat assignments, but for today, I want to start out with an experiment. Forget where you're supposed to sit for the time being—we're going to try something different."

What was that? No seat assignments?

"I'd like everyone to really listen to each other—not only hear their own instrument, but all the different instruments; so just for today, we're going to mix the sections up." Mr. Fernandez waited for this to sink in. "Cellos, go ahead and find a spot in the violin section. Violas, sit anywhere. It's kind of a musical mash-up."

"Find different places, people!" Ms. Patel chirped.

Garrett Goodness raised his hand from the back. "Excuse me, but where did you say we're supposed to go?"

"Anywhere you like." Mr. Fernandez gestured around the room, grinning.

Charlie sank down in the nearest chair. The other kids were cautiously moving around the room looking for seats. Suddenly, a shock of thick brown hair above a smiling face appeared in front of her, along with a cello.

"Hi," Devin said lightly over his shoulder.

"Hey." Charlie exhaled.

Mr. Fernandez tapped his baton on the stand and nodded for rehearsal to begin. They started with some easy scales to warm up and went on to the theme from *Star Wars*. It was impossible to concentrate. Charlie could see Devin's elbow swinging back and forth in front of her, his back swaying with the music. The cello sounded a little like a baritone singing. Every note was rich and full. When they came to a resting spot for the cellos, Devin dropped his bow to one side, while Charlie and the other violins picked up the melody.

All of a sudden, Devin reached into his pocket with his free hand. What the heck—was he pulling out his phone? With a quick twist, he tilted the phone toward her. Charlie swallowed a giggle and skipped three notes. Devin's screen image, barely visible out of the corner of his pocket, was a photograph of a green turtle sitting on top of a cello case! With one hand, Devin deftly typed, while the other arm pulled the bow in front of his cello, as if he was actually playing. To her amazement, Charlie saw Tommy, who was sitting across the room, grin and reach into his own pocket.

At the first pause, Charlie leaned forward. "Nice turtle."

"Thanks," Devin whispered back.

"What's his name?"

"Uh—it's Ludwig, actually."

Charlie sputtered and began coughing as she tried to stifle her laughter. As soon as they took a break, she drew out her own phone and quickly texted Sarah: **News flash: Devin has a turtle and it's named after Beethoven.**

Sarah texted back, **Ha! You could buy a goldfish and call him Amadeus.**

"Anything wrong, Ms. Roth?" Mr. Fernandez peered over

the stand, pointing his baton straight at her. "We're about to start again."

Charlie shook her head. No, nothing wrong at all.

Charlie was still smiling when she got home that afternoon. She made a cup of tea and sat staring out the kitchen window, thinking about Devin's turtle. She wondered whether Nana Rose and Lottie had any pets when they were children and made a note to ask.

Her phone buzzed with a text from Hannah: **At the library with Amy. When are you getting here?**

Charlie smacked her hand to her forehead. She'd made plans to meet her friends at the library at four to work on their research projects. They were supposed to have at least three library books for their bibliographies. Charlie had been so rattled by the mash-up at orchestra practice that she'd completely forgotten. Mom had already left for a meeting, and Dad was still at work. How could she get there? The library was way too far to walk.

Devin's in the reference room, Amy texted.

Charlie sprinted upstairs to where Jake lay sprawled across the floor with his iPad.

"Hey, Jake . . ."

"I'm in the middle of something." He didn't look up.

"I need a ride to the library. I have to do some research for my family history project. It's kind of required."

"You know I don't have my license yet," Jake replied, "not that I would bring you anyway."

"Can't you get a friend to do it?" Charlie bent over and covered the iPad with one hand. "What about that girl with the braids who's obviously got a massive crush on you? She's always picking you up in her car."

Jake scowled. "Not an option. Alison's busy this afternoon." His face softened slightly when he saw Charlie's dark frown. "Well, maybe in a couple of hours, but I can't make any promises."

Charlie groaned. What if she rode her bike? She'd have to go on the parkway, where there was a bike lane, sort of, but with buses and trucks whizzing by, it was fast and dangerous. Mom wouldn't want her anywhere near there, and Dad would probably ground her on the spot if he knew.

A new text from Hannah popped up: **Devin just asked where you are.**

Charlie chewed on the edge of her nail, then nudged Jake's shin with her foot. "If Mom gets back, tell her I'm at Hannah's house, okay?"

"You can go ahead, but there's no way I'm covering for you," Jake grunted.

Charlie got on her bike and pedaled to the entrance of the parkway. She paused to watch the cars zoom by before pulling into the narrow bike lane. She hadn't counted on the thundering noise; every car and truck sounded like it was about to slam into her back tire. The only other bikers were a couple of middle-aged guys in blue spandex who sped past her on their skinny racers.

Breathe, breathe, breathe! A gigantic eighteen-wheeler roared by, then a dump truck rumbled past. Charlie barely exhaled until she saw the exit for the library. When she reached the parking lot, her legs were wobbly and her head hurt like mad.

Charlie swallowed hard, tossed her hair over her shoulder, and marched inside.

"Hey, you made it." Hannah waved. She and Amy were sharing a computer in the reference room.

"Devin just came by," Amy added.

"Did he, um, say anything?" Charlie asked.

"Not this round." Hannah giggled. "But he's walked by three times."

The girls went in different directions to look for books. The librarian steered Charlie to the back corner of the second floor where a section of books was dedicated to the Holocaust.

Suddenly, Charlie noticed a tall figure with a tuft of gray hair at the far end of the room. He was wearing a red plaid jacket and sitting with his back facing her. The man was mumbling loudly.

When he turned his head her way, Charlie realized with a shiver that it was Dr. Szemere, the owner of the awful dog! There was something in his hands. Charlie stretched to see better—was Dr. Szemere holding a camera? He sat hunched over the table, oddly muttering and snapping photos. What was he up to?

"Are you ready?"

Charlie jumped as Amy appeared beside her, books piled high in her arms.

"Shhhhh!" Grabbing the edge of Amy's sweater, Charlie pulled her behind a bookshelf and pointed at Dr. Szemere.

"Isn't that Hannah's neighbor...the one with the nasty dog?" Amy asked.

"Yes, and he's acting strange," Charlie whispered. "Look at the camera! He's talking to himself and taking photos."

"Of what?" Amy asked.

"Books!" Charlie answered.

"Yeah, that *is* weird." The tower of books in Amy's arms suddenly tipped, crashing to the floor. Dr. Szemere's head jerked up. He growled something they couldn't hear, rose from his chair, and hurried away.

"Sorry!" Amy gathered the books from the floor while Charlie peered around the stacks.

She tiptoed over to the table where Dr. Szemere had been sitting. There were five or six pencils, a ruler, and a tape measure lying on top of a large book tagged with pink Post-its. Charlie opened the book to the first Post-it and frowned. The page was filled with drawings of violin bows. One of the bows had intricate mother-of-pearl detailing, just like the one Mr. Fernandez used.

Why would Dr. Szemere be taking pictures of bows? And what was he measuring?

Amy came up from behind and nudged Charlie in the ribs. "Look who's over there."

They could barely make out the top of Devin's head coming up the stairs. When he reached the top step and spotted them, he immediately stopped, checked his pockets, and hastily retreated.

"He definitely likes you," Amy whispered.

"Watch out!" Charlie pushed Amy back behind the stacks just as Dr. Szemere returned. He scowled when he noticed that his book had been opened.

"Do you think he saw us?" Charlie took a deep breath.

Amy shrugged. "We'd better find Hannah."

Hannah was sitting in the library café with a mug of hot chocolate and three slices of banana bread.

"You won't believe this," Charlie said. "We just ran into scary Dr. Szemere."

"He was taking pictures with a camera and talking to himself," Amy added.

Hannah's phone buzzed, and she glanced down at the text. "Mom's here to pick us up. Do you need a ride, Charlie? Our Jeep has a bike rack."

Charlie was about to say yes when she caught sight of Devin at the opposite end of the room. "I forgot to check something!" she blurted out. "You guys go ahead; I'll be fine."

Amy and Hannah grinned at each other as they gathered their things to leave.

"Good luck." Hannah waved. "And text us."

118

CHAPTER TWENTY-ONE

Charlie walked over to where she'd spotted Devin, but he'd already disappeared. She returned to the Holocaust section, chose two books from the shelves, and sat down at a carrel.

The first book had a chart filled with horrifying statistics. Six million people dead. It was such a large number that Charlie could hardly imagine it. What if the entire state of Connecticut was empty? Or nearly all of New York City, simply gone?

One of the photographs showed an enormous pile of shoes left behind by the people who had been killed. Charlie swallowed hard and looked down at her purple sneakers. Thank goodness Nana Rose was safe, but Nathan Kulka's words rang in her head. What were the chances that Lottie, too, had managed to escape a terrible fate?

The next book showed Jewish life in Europe before the war.

This book had pictures of shtetls, small Jewish villages that no longer existed, with narrow dirt streets and wooden huts, cows and donkeys, men in large fur hats and long beards, and women wearing scarves tied at their chins. Charlie lingered over the photo of a rabbi standing with a prayer book in one hand and holding the arm of a young boy with the other. The rabbi's face was dark and serious, but the boy, who wore a long black jacket and a yarmulke on his head, had lips half curled in a shy smile.

The last chapter in the book was about Vienna. There were photographs of grand buildings on wide boulevards, including the main synagogue and the famous Musikverein, the magnificent concert hall where the Vienna Philharmonic played. Charlie paused for a minute, imagining Lottie taking bows beneath the elaborate painted ceiling and crystal chandeliers. Another photo showed a Jewish family at a café decorated with white and gold tiles, hanging brass lamps, and shiny bentwood chairs. The marble counters were stacked with cakes and strudels. Charlie carefully studied every detail and tried to picture Nana Rose and Lottie there as children, chatting in German and drinking hot cocoa with whipped cream.

Charlie wondered whether Lottie had ever gone to a café with Johann Schmidt. Would they have shared a piece of Linzer torte and coffee after a concert? Was Johann very handsome? Did he play the violin, too?

There was still no sign of Devin. Charlie put the book away and sighed. He'd probably already gone home. She stood and checked the rest of the floor.

The spot where Dr. Szemere had been sitting was empty, but Charlie noticed a pink Post-it lying beneath the table and quickly scooped it up. The word *SZEPE* was written in capital letters. What could that could possibly mean? Through the large arched windows behind the table, Charlie saw that the sky had turned a threatening shade of gray; charcoal clouds filled the windowpanes.

Charlie grabbed her backpack and hurried toward the stairs. On the first step, her bag thumped straight into Devin's chest.

"Oh, sorry!" she exclaimed.

"Hey." Devin stopped and leaned against the railing. "Hannah said you might be coming today.... What are you working on?"

"Family history project," Charlie replied.

"Me too." Devin swept the hair from his forehead. "I'm researching my grandpa from Ireland. He played in a band with the Clancy Brothers. Accordion and tin whistle, mostly, but some fiddle as well."

"I love Irish music!" Charlie smiled. "One time I went to an Irish music festival with my dad. I don't know how those guys play so fast."

"Yeah." Devin nodded. "There's no written music; it's mostly based on folk tunes that are handed down. It's even harder than it seems."

It was nice, Charlie thought, really nice, to be talking to a boy about different kinds of music. Especially a boy with green eyes, thick lashes, and perfect pitch.

"I heard about your project." Devin cocked his head with a serious look. "Hannah says you're trying to find your relative. Any luck?"

Before Charlie could answer, a tremendous crack shook the air.

"Was that thunder?" Devin frowned.

"I'd better go." Charlie left Devin on the steps and sprinted through the main reading room, but by the time she got outside, it was pouring. Charlie paused, wondering if there was a bus nearby, or whether she should call Dad at work. He'd be mad, she knew, but how long could she possibly be grounded for going to the library?

All of a sudden, Charlie felt a strong presence surround her, like someone was sneaking up from behind.

"Young lady," a deep voice whispered.

Charlie jumped forward and tripped; her left knee whacked against the wet pavement.

"Young lady!" the voice called again, this time bellowing louder and with an insistent ring.

Charlie glanced over her shoulder as she scrambled to her feet. It was Dr. Szemere. There was no time to think. She fled to her bike as rain pelted against her face. What if Dr. Szemere had seen her spying on him? What would the strange man do?

Finding the library had been easy coming off the parkway; there were lots of signs pointing the way. But now the sky was overcast and filled with shadows, and Charlie wasn't sure where the parkway began. The wind picked up, driving rain into her eyes. She pedaled down the street and made a turn where she thought she was supposed to veer left, but pulled up in front of a broken-down repair shop. Nothing looked familiar. Her knee ached, and it was getting harder and harder to see.

A streak of lightning bolted across the sky. Charlie felt sick; she knew she shouldn't be biking in a storm—one direct hit, and she'd be finished.

Suddenly, a dark blue van came up from behind and started honking. Oh no, was it Dr. Szemere? Charlie pedaled like mad, heart thumping, unsure which way to go. Back to the library? Where was the right street? She thought she could see the parkway somewhere below her, but by now all the cars had their lights on; the entire road glowed like a carnival ride. Charlie felt dizzy and the ground was slick. Another streak of lightning shot across the sky, followed immediately by a horrendous bang.

The van kept honking; it was definitely following her.

Charlie swerved off the street, praying the van would pass. The bike bumped and skidded as it came to a stop. She quickly jumped off, but the van stopped short in front of her. Charlie dropped the bike and hoisted her backpack, ready to run, but just then, a tall boy in a yellow rain jacket climbed out from the passenger side; a slim girl with blond braids and a polka-dot umbrella followed from the driver's seat.

"Jake?" Charlie squinted in the rain.

"Mom's been back for nearly an hour, and she's starting to flip! Why didn't you answer your phone?"

"You covered for me?" Charlie mumbled under her breath. Her heart was still thumping against her ribs.

"I'm Alison." The girl with the braids flashed a crooked smile and held out the umbrella.

"Put your bike in the back of the van," Jake ordered, "before I get soaked. Next time you have one of your stupid ideas, just forget about it, okay?"

"Thanks, Jake. I mean it," Charlie said. She had never, ever, been so glad to see her brother. Ever.

"You owe me," Jake replied. "Big-time."

CHAPTER TWENTY-TWO

That Wednesday after school, Charlie sat at her desk staring at the red binder. The family history report was due the following Monday morning, and her social studies teacher, Mr. Erikson, had announced that he would give no extensions. Although Charlie had written three pages about Lottie's childhood and made exhibits including copies of entries from Lottie's music journal, there was lots more to cover, and she still hadn't started the conclusion section. Mr. Erikson was a stickler for conclusions. But what could she say when so much remained unclear?

Though I did not find my great-aunt Lottie, Charlie finally typed, *I did learn more about my family, and about our family members who died in the Holocaust.* Charlie shifted in her chair, unsure what to write next. She took out a cough drop and decided to check her texts.

There was a new message, but Charlie didn't recognize the number.

Hey. What's up? Remember we talked about doing pit for *West Side Story*? Auditions are in two weeks. Are you in?

Charlie nearly choked. She quickly texted Sarah: **Devin wants me to do pit orchestra for the musical. What should I say?**

Her phone started to ring, and Sarah's name popped up.

"Say *yes!*" Sarah exclaimed before Charlie had a chance to speak. "Obviously! I mean, you like him... don't you?"

"Maybe." Charlie coughed. "But I don't have time to worry about Devin right now. There's something I haven't told you yet." Charlie glanced down at the half-written report.

"What do you mean?" Sarah asked.

"Last weekend, Mom and I went to look for Cousin Nathan at the seniors' home."

"Oh my gosh, Charlie!" Sarah sounded shocked. "Why didn't you tell me? Did you find him?"

"Sort of... at least I think it was him." Charlie exhaled slowly.

"Wow! Did he remember anything?"

"It was weird." Charlie turned and looked at the torn photo of Nathan and Lottie on the bulletin board. "For a minute, he was acting like I *was* Lottie... as if he was talking to her when they were young."

"What did he say?"

"He was all mixed up. He couldn't keep anything straight.

And the *really* weird thing was, he asked me about Johann Schmidt—he wanted to know if Johann had *sent* me there!"

"Wasn't that Lottie's boyfriend?" Sarah asked. "Those were the initials on her necklace, right?"

"I thought so," Charlie replied. "And he's the very last name in Lottie's music journal—they went to a concert together right before the journal ends. But nobody in my family's ever heard of him. When I asked Nana Rose, she said she didn't know whether Lottie had a boyfriend."

"Well, maybe Lottie kept it a secret—maybe she wasn't supposed to date?"

"I guess. Nana told me it was harder for guys and girls to hang out back then." Charlie bit her lip. "But I keep thinking, and I still can't figure this out—how would Cousin Nathan even know Johann? I mean, Lottie lived in Vienna, which is the capital of Austria, and Nathan lived in Budapest, which is in Hungary. Nana Rose said they only visited each other once or twice."

"*Charlie!*" Mom was yelling from downstairs. There was an urgent edge to her voice.

"Gotta go—call you later." Charlie leapt to her feet and opened the door.

"*Charlie!*" Something was definitely wrong.

"What is it?" Charlie came out of her room and peered down the steps. Her mother stood at the bottom waving an envelope.

"This just came in the mail." Mom was breathless. "Come look!"

Charlie hurried down the stairs and studied the envelope. It was manila and sealed with what seemed to be first aid tape.

"Look at the name on the front!" Mom's face was pale, and her hand was shaking.

A shiver went down Charlie's spine. On the top of the envelope someone had scrawled *Lottie* in pencil. A different hand had written their address in pen. The return address was stamped: CONNECTICUT HELPING HOME.

"Do you think...?"

Mom drew a deep breath. "Go ahead and open it, but be careful."

As Charlie tore the envelope open, something shiny clattered to the floor. She dropped to her knees and came back up with a small metal object.

"Let me see," Mom said.

Charlie opened her palm. It was a round silver pendant. When she flipped it over, her heart began to beat out of her chest. Inscribed on the back were two letters: JS.

"What's that?" Mom asked.

"Wait!" Charlie ran back up the stairs and quickly returned carrying the Mogen David necklace from Nana Rose. "Look!" She held the pendants side by side in her hands.

Mom stared at the Star of David. "Is that Lottie's necklace?"

"Yes, and look, they both say JS on the back!"

"JS? I don't get it." Mom frowned.

"Don't you remember? Johann Schmidt was the boy

from Lottie's music journal. Cousin Nathan asked if we knew Johann, too—it must be the same JS!"

Mom's mouth dropped open. "Hurry up—open the rest."

Charlie tore along the edges of the envelope. Two small pieces of thin paper were folded inside. One of the sheets ripped slightly as she pulled it out.

"Be careful." Mom exhaled.

Both sides of each sheet were filled with tiny black script. "These are very old—I think they must be in German." Mom glanced over the first piece of paper.

Charlie picked up the second sheet. *"Mom!"*

"Sweetheart? What is it?"

Charlie pointed to the bottom of the page. The closing and signature were unmistakable:

Deinen Cousin, Lottie.

Mom stared at the name for a moment and then lifted her eyes to meet Charlie's. "It's from Lottie," she whispered. "This is unbelievable! Is there a date?"

They scanned the top of the page.

"Mom—look!" There it was: *Oktober 1945.*

Mom gasped. "This is dated October, but by then, the war had already ended. The letter was written *after* the war was over!"

Charlie couldn't swallow. She was startled to see that her mother's eyes were glistening, then welling with tears.

"Lottie must have...For goodness' sakes, Charlie, *you've found her!*"

129

Mom eased down on the stairs, rubbing her wet cheeks. "Lottie survived the war. She was alive, but they thought... the whole family thought that..." Mom wiped the corners of her eyes and shook her head.

"I'll be right back!" Charlie took the letter, picked up her backpack, and rushed toward the front door.

"Wait, where are you going?"

"Amy's house—keep your fingers crossed that her grandma's home." Two fingers entwined above her head, Charlie ran for her bike.

 130

CHAPTER TWENTY-THREE

Charlie hooted in triumph as she quickly pedaled toward Amy's house. The truth was sitting right there in her backpack. If Lottie had survived, if she hadn't been killed like the millions of other Jewish children, it would truly be a Nana Rose epic miracle. Charlie licked her lips and pushed even harder. Could Lottie still be living? That would be the best present she could ever give Nana Rose. To see her again, after all those years! Lottie would look older, of course, but Nana would still recognize her sister's mischievous smile. Perhaps she would even be able to play her violin; Charlie had seen a program on TV about elderly people who still played music every day.

The shabby brown house on the corner came into view, and Charlie glanced around nervously. She still wasn't sure what Dr. Szemere was doing taking pictures at the library, and there was no way she was going to risk being chased by his scary dog again. Luckily, the house seemed perfectly quiet; if anything, it had a slightly abandoned air, like a dollhouse that hadn't been put away. She heard a noise and clutched the handlebars—was that barking? No, it was only the mail truck rounding the corner behind her.

Charlie dropped her bike in front of Amy's door and raced up the steps, panting, as she pressed the buzzer once, twice, three times. Nana Klein had to be home, she just had to be.

"Charlie! Is that you?" Mrs. Klein answered the door.

"Hi—what's up?" Amy scooted in from the kitchen.

"I need your help!" Charlie bent over to catch her breath. "Something incredible came in the mail. A cousin sent us an old letter in German. I was hoping your nana could read it."

"Come right in, Charlie." Mrs. Klein motioned her inside. "Though I think my mother may be sleeping."

"It's okay! It's fine!" A high-pitched voice rang out. "I'm over here, girls—come and see me!" Nana Klein sat on the family room couch, her thin legs sticking out from under a white crocheted blanket. She raised her hands and reached forward. "Charlie, dear, what have you got there? More about your relative, the one who was lost in the Holocaust?"

Nana Klein was wearing bright red lipstick that wasn't entirely on her lips, but her hands were soft and warm.

"She might be alive," Charlie said breathlessly. "Well, at least we think it's possible. I brought a letter for you to read—I hope you're not too tired...?" Charlie hurriedly pulled out the sheets. "Cousin Nathan sent it. This is her signature—Lottie—and look, it's from October 1945!"

"Whoa." Amy cocked her head sideways. "But Charlie...I don't get it. How does that change anything? That's still a long, long time ago."

"Well, yeah—it's old. But the important thing is, this letter was written *after* World War Two ended," Charlie quickly replied.

"It means your great-aunt wasn't killed!" Mrs. Klein exclaimed. "She didn't die in the camps like your family thought."

Nana Klein clapped her hands together, nodding vigorously. "It is possible; I know of other cases. There was utter confusion after the war; so many families were separated. You cannot imagine it! Mothers and fathers and children came out from their hiding places and searched for each other, but sometimes, people didn't even know where to look." Nana Klein smiled sadly. "May I see that correspondence now?"

Charlie's head felt light. This was it. What would Lottie's letter say? Would it reveal what had happened to her after the war?

Nana Klein carefully picked up the first sheet. The fragile paper shook as she held it to the light. She squinted and wiped her eyes. "I need my glasses, please."

Charlie hopped from one foot to the other while she waited for Nana Klein to place her glasses on her nose and begin, her red lips moving silently. *"Oy!"* Nana Klein said under her breath. She reached for the second sheet.

Amy elbowed Charlie, thumbs up.

I think I can! I think I can! What book was that from? Of course, *The Little Engine That Could!* All of a sudden, Charlie couldn't get it out of her head. Did the kind blue engine make it to the top of the mountain? Why couldn't she remember?

Finally, Nana Klein stacked the sheets of paper in her lap and took off her glasses, while Charlie held her breath.

"I apologize, Charlie, I can't help you," Nana Klein said.

"What?" Charlie's heart was free-falling into her stomach.

"I'm very sorry, but I cannot read this letter."

"Are you sure? Is the writing too small?"

"No, that's not the problem, though my eyes aren't so good anymore." Nana Klein shook her head slowly. "The trouble is, this isn't German."

"Not German? But Mom told me it was . . ."

"Yes, I see the date and a few German words at the end. But the rest is in a different language entirely."

"What language?" Mrs. Klein asked.

"This is Magyar," Nana Klein said in a matter-of-fact tone.

"Mud-yar?" Amy stared at the sheets of paper. "What's that?"

"It's in Hungarian," Nana Klein replied. "Didn't you say your great-aunt moved to Budapest?"

Charlie caught her breath and nodded.

"You see, people went back and forth in those days

134

between Austria and Hungary; the two countries were linked. Many people had relatives in both places and spoke both languages. If Lottie spent the war years in Hungary, she must have learned Hungarian."

"But Nana, are you sure you can't read it?" Amy saw the crushed expression on Charlie's face.

"No, I'm afraid I cannot—oh, long ago, when I was young, maybe, I could make out a few words, but I am sorry to say, you'll have to find someone else." Nana Klein sighed. "I wish I could help you. I think you'll find a way. If at first you don't succeed, you must try, try again, you know."

"My nana says that, too." Charlie managed a weak smile.

"Maybe you have some other Hungarian relatives?" Mrs. Klein asked.

"No, not really." Charlie imagined bringing the letters back to Cousin Nathan at the seniors' home. It wouldn't help, she knew.

"Perhaps someone at school?"

Charlie shrugged. She doubted that the Spanish and Chinese teachers would also be fluent in Magyar.

"Do you want to hang out here?" Amy asked. "It might make you feel better. We could chill in my room and talk. Or listen to music—whatever you want."

"I can't." Charlie was suddenly exhausted. "I should go. My mom will want to know what I found out."

"I'm terribly sorry I couldn't help you, my dear." Nana Klein leaned forward, one hand across her chest. "You have so much feeling in your heart. You will find your great-aunt Lottie, I know you will."

"Good luck," Mrs. Klein added.

"Thanks, anyway." Charlie lifted the backpack on her shoulder and trudged out the front door. Her head was pounding with disappointment as she got on her bike and coasted down the driveway.

Charlie pedaled slowly and anxiously along the street, zigzagging around cracks and stray branches. What now? How could she possibly find someone quickly to translate Lottie's letter? Perhaps she could see if her Hebrew school teacher knew of another refugee—someone who spoke Hungarian?

Up ahead, she saw Dr. Szemere's house. What was Satan's real name, again? If Satan gave chase, maybe she could calm the dog down by using her actual name. Kinga . . . wasn't it? Of course! Kinga, the Puli.

Whoa! Kinga the *Hungarian* Puli.

Dr. Szemere had said he was Hungarian, too.

Pumping one fist to the sky, Charlie filled her lungs and raced toward Dr. Szemere's. "I think I can; I think I can!" she sang out into the breeze.

CHAPTER TWENTY-FOUR

When Charlie reached Dr. Szemere's driveway, she stopped short, caught her breath, and strained to listen. Sure enough, muffled barking was coming from somewhere on the property. But she couldn't see the dog. If she was lucky, Kinga was locked in the house. Charlie pulled a handful of hair clips from her backpack and set down the bike. At least she could pelt those in Kinga's direction if the threatening dog approached.

The barking stopped, and Charlie took a few hesitant steps toward the house. She could feel her pulse throbbing. Even if she escaped being mauled, what about Dr. Szemere? He was definitely a bit strange. Why had he chased after her at the library? Could he be dangerous, too? Charlie swallowed hard. There was absolutely no choice. She had to know what was in Lottie's letter—*right now.*

Charlie headed cautiously toward the porch. All of a sudden, she heard a spine-chilling snarl. She jumped back, but with a flood of relief, she saw that Kinga was tied to a tree at the side of the house. The dog growled and lunged forward against the leash but couldn't get near her.

She climbed the stairs to the porch slowly, pausing on each step. Charlie's heart was pounding in her ears as she rang the bell. Maybe she should have gone back to Amy's and asked her to come along. She pulled out her phone and scrolled to Jake's number, just in case she had to call him, fast. Finally, she rang the doorbell, breathing hard: Should she get out of there while she still could?

But nobody answered the door.

Kinga stopped growling and began to whine, and after a few minutes, lay down with a yawn. Charlie shook her head. Silly dog!

On the porch, a wicker bench was set against the house, and next to it was a small window. The shade was drawn low, but Charlie noticed a narrow gap at the bottom. She took off her helmet and set it down. Then, cupping her hands on the glass, she peered into the house—and quickly sprang back to one side. Dr. Szemere was in there!

Charlie stood sideways beside the window and bench, trying to make herself smaller. After taking a deep breath, she leaned over and peeked in again. Dr. Szemere was bent low over what looked to be his kitchen table. She could see a chisel in his hands, but she couldn't make out what he was working on. He wore headphones and goggles and had on the same plaid jacket he'd been wearing at the library. On the wall above the table, there was a large framed poster of a magnificent white horse rearing on its hind legs.

Dr. Szemere suddenly looked up and their eyes met. His lips formed a tight O as he sprang to his feet. Charlie clutched her backpack, unsure whether to stay or run. Before she could decide, the door swung open.

"Do you require something, young lady?" Dr. Szemere loomed in front of her. The headphones were down around his neck, and Charlie could hear music. It was a Viennese waltz, she realized. One of Nana Rose's favorites.

"I—I'm Charlie Roth. Do you remember me? I was here before."

"The girl from the library, yes," Dr. Szemere replied. "I attempted to offer you a ride in the rain, but you ran away."

"Oh, I'm sorry, I didn't understand!" Charlie's face was tingling with embarrassment. Would he still help her after the rude way she'd behaved? "Dr. Szemere, I need to ask you a favor."

"What is it?" Dr. Szemere looked at his watch, then pointed at the bench beside the window. He motioned for Charlie to sit.

"You said you were from Hungary," Charlie began, "when I was here the last time—that is, when Satan—"

Dr. Szemere frowned.

"Oops! I mean Kinga," Charlie said quickly. "I got the name mixed up with another dog, a really big, angry dog—"

There was a slight twitch at the corner of Dr. Szemere's mouth. "Kinga enjoys barking, I'm afraid. As you well know."

"Yes," Charlie said, glancing at the yard. "My question is... can you read Hungarian? I mean, could you possibly translate a letter for me?"

The outermost edges of Dr. Szemere's lips twitched again. "Most children have never heard of my native country and language, nor have any interest in it. Why do you ask?"

"It's kind of a long story," Charlie said.

Dr. Szemere sat on the bench next to Charlie and nodded. "Go ahead."

"Okay.... Well, my grandmother's sister was living in Budapest when she was a teenager—she was a student at the music academy. Then the war came, and she completely disappeared." Charlie paused. "I'm doing a school project about her." Dr. Szemere looked as though he might be impressed by the idea of schoolwork. "Now we've found an old letter she wrote, but it's in Hungarian, and I can't read it."

"When exactly did this girl reside in Budapest?"

"She moved there right before World War Two. She was an amazing violinist, maybe you've heard of her? Her name was Charlotte Kulka, but everyone called her Lottie."

"I am not quite so old," Dr. Szemere replied. "I was a boy in the 1950s when my family came to America."

"Oh... of—of course," Charlie stammered. "I'm sorry."

"Your relative was Hungarian?" Dr. Szemere pursed his lips.

"No." Charlie shook her head. "The family was from Vienna."

"They were Jewish, perhaps?" he asked.

Charlie nodded. "My nana and her mother escaped to America, but Lottie wasn't with them—she was still in Budapest."

"And so, the girl was in grave danger," Dr. Szemere concluded.

"They never heard from Lottie again, and everyone thought she was probably dead—though nobody knew for sure. But now, a very old cousin sent us this letter, and if you look at the date . . . it turns out that Lottie was alive at the end of the war!" Charlie's face brightened for a moment.

"Show the letter to me, please."

Charlie reached into her backpack and pulled out the thin sheets. It was quiet in the yard; Kinga had fallen asleep under the tree. Dr. Szemere scanned the pages, his lips moving slightly. He began to read aloud:

My dear Nathan,

How wonderful it is to receive your letter from America! But also sad to know that your parents did not survive. It must have been difficult for you to go on the ship to the United States all alone.

"Poor Cousin Nathan!" Charlie whispered.

I have heard nothing these years from my own parents, but a friend from Vienna wrote that my father was arrested. My dear music teacher, Herr Hinkleman, is also gone. Now that we know the

terrible truth about the Nazis, I'm afraid that my family is forever
lost. It hurts most that they took little Rose. I can never forgive this.

Charlie's stomach tightened to a knot. Lottie thought
Nana Rose had been killed! If only Lottie had known what
really happened.

"Should I continue?" Dr. Szemere paused with a sideways
glance.

Charlie exhaled and nodded.

I am lucky, though, to also have happy news, the best news, to
tell you. Here in Budapest, I met a special boy. His name is Istvan
Bartos. His family is Catholic. Istvan's father was killed in the
fighting, but his mother and sister hid me during the last year of the
war, although they knew I was Jewish and would have risked their
lives had I been discovered.

Now we are married. Even better news, we expect a baby!

"A baby!" Charlie blurted out. "Lottie has a baby?"

"Apparently," said Dr. Szemere, looking up. "But consider
the child would not be a baby now. He would be an adult; perhaps my age or even older."

"Oh, gosh, I guess that's right." Charlie rubbed her head.
There was so much to consider. Lottie had married a boy
named Istvan, and not Johann Schmidt as she had imagined.

Dr. Szemere continued:

We hope to come to the United States, but Istvan wants to wait until our baby has grown strong. Then we will come.

"Wait—what did you say?" Charlie jumped to her feet. "Lottie came to America? Lottie is *here*?"

"Well," Dr. Szemere said, examining the letter again, "it says that your relative *wished* to come to America—but they intended to wait some time."

"Then they *must* be here!" Charlie exclaimed.

Dr. Szemere shook his head. "I'm afraid it would not be that simple. The letter is dated October 1945. If they waited *too* long to come, you see, then it would have been impossible."

"What do you mean?" Charlie asked.

"The communists took control of Hungary in 1948. After that, the borders were closed. The so-called Iron Curtain prevented anyone from leaving the country. There was very little communication, because the communists searched correspondence."

"But *you* moved to America, didn't you?"

"In 1956, yes, there was a short period for escape, when Hungary revolted and tried to break free." Dr. Szemere sighed. "But there was not another opportunity to leave like that again until the fall of the Soviet Union in 1989."

"I guess we learned something about that at school," Charlie said, wishing she knew more.

Dr. Szemere cleared his throat and continued translating.

Perhaps someday soon I will see you again! Istvan has relatives in Cleveland—is that far from Connecticut? I have been told there is a very fine symphony there. Not as fine as the orchestras of Europe perhaps, but I pray that I can play music there once more. We were forced to sell my violin during the war, but Istvan says he has managed to put aside a little money and will soon buy me another.

My dearest Nathan, I wish you a wonderful life in America! You will be a big success as a dentist, I am sure of it. When you think of all we've endured, take heart. We saved many.

Your loving cousin,
Lottie

"So, your great-aunt was a very lucky person," Dr. Szemere observed. "She was able to survive, as you hoped."

Charlie smiled for a second, then frowned. She still had so many questions. "What does she mean when she says they saved many?"

Dr. Szemere shrugged and stood up. "Come inside for one moment, please; there is something I would like to show you."

He led her into the kitchen, where he'd just been working. When she peered at the table, Charlie couldn't believe her eyes. It was covered with sticks of wood, what appeared to be strands of horsehair, and carving tools. The enlarged photograph of a violin bow lay next to the chisel.

"What is all this?" Charlie asked.

Dr. Szemere lowered his voice. "My father was a luthier in Hungary. He made magnificent violins, violas, and cellos, as did his father before him. His violins, especially, were renowned throughout Europe. But when the Russians invaded in 1956, all hope for our country was crushed. We left our village and crossed the border in the middle of the night. My father was forced to abandon his workshop and had to leave everything behind."

"Couldn't your dad make violins in America?" Charlie asked.

"I am afraid there was little demand for such fine pieces, and nobody recognized his gift. In the end, my father repaired cheap instruments, and my mother cleaned office buildings to support our family and pay for my medical education."

Charlie gazed at the materials on the table. "But you—"

"I make only the bows." Dr. Szemere looked away for a moment. "It keeps me occupied since my wife passed away."

He went into the next room and returned with a slender, elegant bow. "You play the violin, just like your relative; am I correct?"

"How did you guess that?" Charlie asked.

Dr. Szemere didn't answer; he held up the bow. "This one seems as if it might suit you. But we will have to see. You know that violinists never choose their bows, not really—the bow chooses them."

"It's wonderful!" Charlie sighed as she admired the handsome wooden bow. "But I—I don't think I can take this. My parents wouldn't want me to accept anything so valuable."

"This is not a gift," Dr. Szemere replied. "Only a loan. The bow must be tested with an instrument; you will return it to me whenever you like."

Charlie took the bow in her hands. The wood was light and perfectly balanced, the horsehair smooth to the touch. It was absolutely gorgeous.

"Siberian horsehair is of course the finest." Dr. Szemere straightened his shoulders with pride as he nodded toward the poster of the white stallion on the wall.

"Thank you," Charlie said softly.

Dr. Szemere placed the bow in a slim case, which Charlie carefully slid into her backpack. She couldn't wait to show the bow to Mr. Fernandez and everyone in orchestra.

"One last thing," Dr. Szemere said. "Kinga is not such a bad dog as some may think. When you return, I shall properly introduce you."

Charlie nodded and stepped outside. She quickly walked by Kinga, who lifted her head slightly before dropping it down again.

As she leapt onto her bike, Charlie broke into a wide grin. Lottie might still be alive! She had married and even had a child. But where was Lottie now?

Charlie was determined to find out.

CHAPTER TWENTY-FIVE

"Mom!" Charlie hollered as she flew into the house. She stopped short, realizing the house was quiet. "Mom? Dad?...Jake, are you here?" She ran upstairs and pounded on Jake's door.

"What is it?" Jake peeked his head out.

"Where are Mom and Dad?" Charlie panted.

"Dad's still at work, and Mom had to run out to a meeting. She said she'd be back as soon as she can. What's up?"

"I have something incredible to tell you all! And right now, I need your help." Charlie grabbed Jake by his shirt and pulled him across the hall into her room.

"Okay, but could you make it quick? I'm supposed to meet Alison at the library soon." Jake grinned.

"Listen to me, Jake. I might have found Lottie!"

"What?" Jake exclaimed. "Where? Where is she?"

"Well, I guess I haven't *exactly* found her, but I'm super

close. Nathan Kulka sent me an old letter that Lottie wrote *after* the war, so it turns out she didn't die in the Holocaust like everyone thought! But the terrible thing is, Lottie believed her whole family had been killed—she never knew that her mom and Nana Rose escaped."

"Slow down and tell me what happened. From the beginning." Jake's face was serious now.

"Okay." Charlie took a deep breath. "I got something in the mail from Nathan Kulka today. It was a letter Lottie had written to him in 1945! The letter was in Hungarian, but I had it translated—"

"How'd you manage that?" Jake interrupted her.

"You know Hannah's neighbor, the one with the scary dog?" Charlie paused. "Well, I met him! His name is Dr. Szemere, and I found out that he's Hungarian. So I asked him to translate for me."

"Seriously?" Jake flashed his sister a look of respect she'd never seen from him before.

"Yeah, seriously!" Charlie smiled. "Anyway, it turns out that Lottie was stuck the whole time in Hungary. After the war, she got married to a boy named Istvan Bartos, and they had a baby! She wanted to come to America, but she couldn't, because the Soviets took over.... At least, that's what I think happened."

Jake lifted one eyebrow and whistled. "Are you sure?"

"Well, not exactly . . . but it makes sense, doesn't it? Lottie's letter says that Istvan had relatives in Cleveland. So, I'm guessing they might have come over here, you know, later on when the Soviets left Hungary and people were able to go."

"Hold on a second." Jake scratched his head. "You're telling me you're sort of hoping that once the Soviet Union crumbled, Lottie and her family moved to *Cleveland*?"

"Yes—unless you have a better idea!" Charlie nodded. "I know it's a long shot, but we have to find them! And I'm asking for your help. Where should we start?"

"Well...we start with me telling Alison I'm gonna be late." Jake sent a quick text. "Okay, so what have you tried? Did you check Facebook?"

"I haven't tried anything yet, Jake, I just got home!"

"Right. Let me do this." Jake grabbed Charlie's laptop and did a quick search, but nothing came up. "I dunno." He set the laptop down and rubbed the back of his neck. "I guess we've struck out."

"Wait, I'll ask Sarah." Charlie took out on her phone. "She might have an idea."

Sarah instantly texted back: **Try online directory for Cleveland?**

"Good thinking!" Charlie answered aloud. She picked up the laptop, pulled up a directory site, and typed in *Bartos* and *Cleveland*. A long list of names appeared.

"There's nobody named Istvan or Lottie there." Jake peered over her shoulder at the results.

"But look, there's an R. Bartos." Charlie pointed at the very last name. "Let's try that number first."

"How come?" Jake asked.

"It's only a hunch, but I was named after Nana's sister, Lottie, and Nana's name is..."

"Rose." Jake finished her thought. "So maybe, just *maybe*... Lottie named the baby after her?" Jake lifted one fist and bumped knuckles with Charlie. "Another long shot...but who knows? Let's see!"

"Will you make the call? I'm too nervous." Charlie handed Jake her phone.

"Sure." Jake hit the numbers while Charlie covered her eyes with both hands and waited.

"Hello there." Jake spoke in a low voice. "I was just wondering—who is this?"

Peering between her fingers in dismay, Charlie watched as Jake shook his head.

"Too bad," Jake said. "She hung up."

"Of course she did!" Charlie exclaimed. "You can't just call people out of the blue and then ask who's there! It's creepy."

"Fine, you do it." Jake held the phone in front of her.

"I don't think I can... I'm too scared." Charlie backed away.

"Come on, sis. You've been working on this for weeks. Go ahead and try." Jake redialed the number and pressed the phone to Charlie's ear.

"Hello?" The young woman on the line sounded wary. "Did you call here before?"

"I—I'm sorry, that was my brother," Charlie began. "I'm calling you again because there's a special person we're looking for—"

"I think you have the wrong number." The woman cut her off.

"Wait—please don't hang up! There's something I need to ask." Charlie drew a sharp breath. "Are you related to a Lottie Kulka?"

"I don't believe so . . . ." the woman answered.

"What about Lottie Bartos?" Charlie continued. "Or maybe Istvan Bartos?"

There was silence on the other end of the line. Charlie could hear the woman breathing.

"Do you mean Izzy Bartos?"

"Izzy? I guess he might have called himself that in America." Charlie held one thumb halfway up. Jake's eyes opened wide.

"Izzy Bartos is my grandfather," the woman said.

"Your grandfather!" Charlie raised her thumb higher. "I was wondering if your name is Rose? I mean, the phone listing said *R*."

"No, it's not Rose. Look, I don't know who you are, but if this is a prank call—"

"I swear this isn't a prank call!" Charlie exclaimed. "We're looking for a lost relative. Rose is a family name, so I thought the *R* might be for that."

"The *R* stands for *Rita*—my mother. This is my parents' house."

"Oh, I see." Charlie sighed.

"Now please excuse me; I have to go." The phone clicked, and the line went dead.

"She hung up on me, too!" Charlie frowned at Jake, her head throbbing.

"We should check the other listings." He shrugged.

"But Jake, I *felt* something!" Charlie insisted. "I know it doesn't make any sense, but that woman's voice—even though I've never heard it before—she sounded *familiar*."

They sat in silence for a moment. Then Charlie's phone began to ring. The number Jake had just dialed came up on the screen.

"Hello, hi?" Charlie answered, her throat tight.

"I just asked my mother, and you're right, Grandpa Izzy was actually named Istvan—it's a Hungarian name. He was from Budapest—although he never talked very much about that."

Charlie's heart skipped two beats. "Could you tell me quickly, please—are they still alive?"

"They?" the young woman repeated. "Who are you looking for?"

"Istvan—and his wife, Lottie."

"Well, Grandpa Izzy died last year."

"Oh no!" The phone suddenly felt so heavy that Charlie could barely hold it to her ear. "That's terrible."

"He was very old and lived a full life. I didn't know my grandmother because she passed away a long time ago."

"What?" Charlie froze.

"My grandmother died giving birth to my father, so I never met her."

Charlie looked up at Lottie's photo on the bulletin board. It suddenly seemed faded and far away. "Are—are you positive? You're absolutely certain your grandma died?"

"Yes. She passed away in Europe, soon after the end of World War Two. So it was a long time ago. But I still think you have the wrong family because my grandmother's name wasn't Lottie. I mean, I don't *believe* she was ever called that...."

Charlie inhaled. "Are you sure?"

"Well—her name was Charlotte. In fact, I was named after her...I am Charlotte Bartos."

Gasping for air, Charlie watched as the phone, Jake, the room, all went wavy and blurry and then wavy again.

"Are you crying?" Jake whispered. "What's going on? What did she say?"

"I—I have to tell you something important," Charlie said hoarsely into the phone as she wiped the tears from her cheeks. "My grandmother Rose had a beautiful sister who played the violin and loved music more than anything. Her name was Charlotte Kulka, but her family called her Lottie. And when she disappeared in Hungary during the war, everyone *thought* she died in the Holocaust." Charlie choked; now she could barely speak. "But the thing is, it turns out that Lottie wasn't killed after all. She managed to survive. She married Istvan Bartos, and they had a baby."

"Who *are* you?" The young woman sounded breathless now, too.

"I'm your cousin, Charlie Roth—and I've been looking for you."

CHAPTER TWENTY-SIX

Charlie woke up late Sunday morning with her laptop and red binder still on the pillow where she'd fallen asleep working on her family history report. Yesterday evening, the whole family had Skyped with Charlotte Bartos and her parents. Through smiles and many tears they'd learned more from Lottie's son, Arpad, about his family's life in Hungary and their eventual move to Cleveland.

The report was due at school tomorrow morning, and Charlie couldn't wait to finish.

She had stayed up half the night writing about Nana Rose and her sister, Lottie, growing up in Vienna before the Second World War, and how Lottie had been such an accomplished violinist that she'd performed with the Vienna Philharmonic before going to Budapest to study music. And then, the terrible part—that during the Holocaust, Nana Rose's father had been deported and killed, while Nana Rose and her mother managed to escape to the United States. Since Lottie was still in Hungary, she was tragically left behind. While Nana Rose and her mother always hoped that Lottie had survived, they realized she was probably gone forever. But even though Lottie had been lost, she was never, ever forgotten.

Next, Charlie wrote how Nana Rose had sent her Lottie's music journal and given her the precious gift of Lottie's necklace, and about the mystery surrounding Johann Schmidt. Charlie smiled to herself as she explained how she'd managed to find Cousin Nathan at the seniors' home in Greenfield and how he had sent her the astonishing letter from Lottie that had finally led her to discover Lottie's family in Cleveland.

At last, Charlie stretched her arms, smiled one more time at the photo of Lottie and Nathan on her bulletin board, and began typing her conclusion.

SOCIAL STUDIES, Mr. Erikson—Period 6
Searching for Lottie by Charlie Roth

CONCLUSION

Even though I never got to meet my great-aunt Lottie, I did discover many things about her. The very best part was that she didn't die in the Holocaust like our family always thought. After the war, Lottie stayed in Budapest and married an engineer named Istvan Bartos. Sadly, Lottie believed that everyone in her family had been killed and never found out that her mother and younger sister,

Rose, had escaped to America. Poor Lottie died giving birth to a baby boy named Arpad, but many years later, Istvan and Arpad came to the United States and settled down in Cleveland. Istvan raised his son to be Jewish in loving memory of Lottie, and Arpad became an architect. Arpad married a woman named Rita, whose family had survived the Holocaust hidden in the Hungarian countryside near Lake Balaton. When Arpad and Rita had a baby girl, they named her Charlotte—just like me!

Our "new" cousin Charlotte and her parents are planning to visit us at Hanukkah. Nana Rose will fly up from Florida, and we will have a big family reunion. Mom has made arrangements with the people who run the Connecticut Helping Home for Seniors in Greenfield so we can go together to see our other cousin, Nathan Kulka. I will play a Mozart piece on my violin, and we will bring him apple strudel and potato latkes.

There is only one part of the mystery that I was not able to solve, and it might have gotten even bigger: Who was Johann Schmidt and why did Cousin Nathan have a pendant with the inscription JS on the back that matched the inscription on Lottie's Star of David necklace? Cousin Charlotte didn't recognize Johann's name, but even stranger, it turns out that her grandfather, Lottie's beloved husband, Istvan, left her a pendant when he died with the same inscription on the back—JS! She will bring this along at Hanukkah to show me.

I still wonder: Was Johann Schmidt Lottie's first boyfriend—or could he be another long-lost relative? I will not give up until someday I can figure out this last mystery in our family.

Charlie hit Print on her laptop and set it aside with a contented sigh. Then, with a happy grin, she texted Sarah: **PROJECT DONE!! Thanks for all your help!**

Sarah messaged back with a long line of xo's: **Let's have a sleepover soon to celebrate!! I want to hear about your new cousins!**

The following Saturday, Charlie carefully took the photograph of Lottie with her violin down from her bulletin board. A few days ago, after she'd turned in her report, Dad had given her a silver picture frame.

"Early bat mitzvah gift," Dad said with a hug.

Now Charlie unwrapped the frame and set Lottie's photo inside. The silver made Lottie's dark hair shine. Charlie placed the photograph on her shelf next to a new picture of Arpad and Cousin Charlotte that Rita Bartos had sent. Arpad was tall, with a strong, square jaw and jet-black hair. Cousin Charlotte had short, curly brown hair and the same mischievous smile as Lottie, Charlie thought.

She pulled out her phone to text Sarah: **When should we have our sleepover?**

A minute later, the phone rang, and Charlie put it to her ear without looking. "Hi, Sarah, can you come here next weekend?"

"Um—this is Devin, actually."

"Oh!" Charlie's cheeks flared red; she was super glad he couldn't see her.

"I was just wondering . . . I wanted to know if you were still planning to do pit orchestra for the musical. The auditions are Tuesday."

"Oh, gosh, I completely forgot!" Charlie exclaimed.

"That's okay." Devin coughed into the phone. "It sounds like maybe you're not exactly interested?"

"Oh—no," Charlie quickly replied. "I mean, I am, yeah—I am totally interested. Definitely!"

"The auditions are right after school. Do you maybe want to hang out afterward?"

"Cool. Sure." She grinned and twirled on her toes.

"Sweet. See you then." Devin hung up.

Charlie was just about to text Sarah, Hannah, and Amy when the doorbell rang. "Hey, Jake!" she yelled into the hallway. "Can you go downstairs and see who's at the door?"

The bell rang again and then a third time. Charlie stuck her phone in her pocket and ran downstairs. Through the window she could see the mailman lugging an oversized box back to his truck.

"I'm here!" Charlie opened the door wide.

"Oh, hello—it's the musician." The mailman smiled and returned with the large box and a clipboard for her to sign.

"What's this?" Charlie asked. The box stood nearly halfway to her chin.

"I don't know," the mailman replied, "but it's stamped

'fragile,' and it's heavy, so there must be something important inside for you."

"This is for me?" It wasn't a holiday or Charlie's birthday; she couldn't imagine who would be sending her a gift.

She turned the box over and dragged it into the front hall. Her name and address were printed on the label, and in the lower corner, she noticed a short note: *We all agreed this should be yours.*

Charlie fetched a pair of scissors and cut the box open. Something big was covered in layers of bubble wrap and brown paper. She slowed down and carefully tore away the wrappings. When she saw what was inside, she stepped back, trembling.

Jake appeared at the top of the stairs. "Hey, who was at the door?"

"Wait," Charlie commanded. She reached into the box and pulled out an old leather case.

"What's that?" Jake demanded.

"Not sure." Carefully unclipping the rusted latches, Charlie lifted the cover and peered inside. A violin lay on matted red satin. She touched the top of the instrument with her fingertips, then slowly took it from the case. The wood was smooth and finely carved; the back of the violin was etched with a dark maple flame. Squinting through the f-holes, Charlie could make out a yellowed label: CSINÁLTA *SZEMERE*.

Jake came bounding down the stairs.

"Hold on." Charlie slid her fingers along the soft satin

bottom and pried opened a small compartment. A folded piece of brown cardboard cut in the shape of a heart was wedged behind an ancient chunk of crumbling rosin.

"Open it," Jake said.

Charlie unfolded the faded cardboard. A spark skipped across her shoulders and down her spine and into her heart.

Charlotte, szeretlek, Istvan. She showed the note to Jake. The corners of Charlie's eyes were beginning to well up with tears.

"What does it mean?"

"It means this belonged to Lottie," Charlie answered softly. She looked down at the instrument and whispered, "This is your new violin, isn't it? The one that Istvan promised you after the war, when you were going to have your baby, Arpad."

Charlie wiped her eyes with a sleeve. She darted into the living room and returned with her new bow. Carefully lifting the violin, she placed the instrument against her shoulder. The wood felt smooth as silk. The violin floated between her chin and left hand as she tuned.

Standing on tiptoes, Charlie pulled the bow across the strings. The tone was clear and mellow, unlike any violin she had ever played. She began with the first part of a Beethoven sonata, switched to a Strauss waltz, and ended in a flurry of Mozart. The sweet sound rose into the hallway, up the stairs, through the ceiling.

Without even thinking, Charlie hadn't missed a note, not a single one. How was that possible? She stopped and looked at Jake.

"Not bad!" Jake grinned at Charlie and whistled. "Not bad at all."

Mom sounded breathless as she came down the stairs with Dad right behind her. "I was on the phone, did you answer the door?"

"What's going on?" Dad asked. "What was that fantastic music?"

"Come here, you'll never believe this!" Charlie exclaimed. "Cousin Charlotte and her family sent me Lottie's violin."

"Was that *you* playing?" Mom gasped. "I've never heard you play like that."

"It was me." Charlie beamed. The beautiful violin rested on her arm. She glanced over the smooth wood, the maple flame, and the delicate scrollwork. With a little smile, she added softly, "Me—and maybe, just maybe, a tiny bit of Lottie, too."

Budapest, December 1944

Lottie pulled herself up off the simple wooden cot and rubbed her hands. She peered out the window of the tiny shed to the gnarled grapevines bent along a sloping field. Chunks of dirty snow stuck to the fence separating the field from an orchard of skeleton apple and plum trees.

Lottie had been hiding in the Buda Hills for several weeks. Jews in Hungary had been rounded up into ghettos, but with false identity papers, Lottie had found refuge with the Bartos family, who took her into their small apartment in Budapest despite the great risk. Over time, her bond with the son, Istvan, had grown deeper. Now, with so many Jews being hunted down and deported, Lottie worried that staying in the apartment would threaten the Bartoses' safety, so she had taken shelter in an old shed set in a garden plot above the city.

Dusk was falling, and far below, Lottie could see the twinkling lights of Budapest. She buttoned her worn jacket and tamed her long dark curls into a braid that reached her waist. Shivering, she sat on the bed to wait. A few moments later, she heard a rap at the door.

"Istvan!" Lottie lifted the bar across the door made of splintered boards and rushed into the young man's arms. Istvan's round face beamed with pleasure as they kissed. But then he looked worried.

"You ought to be more careful, my love! Don't ever open the door like that without asking who it is."

"I knew it was you."

"Still, it's not safe. Come..." Istvan took her hand, kissed her again, and then led her carefully down the steep pebbled path in front of the shed.

"Any news?" Lottie asked eagerly.

"Very little. We've had to bury the radio for days. The police searched the apartment again. But we know the Allies are gaining ground; the war cannot last much longer."

"How I wish it would end!" Lottie exclaimed.

"We must take care. It's more dangerous for you now than ever."

"Any word of Herr Hinkleman?" Lottie looked carefully at Istvan's open face.

"No," he said firmly. "Nothing."

"Please don't lie to me," Lottie said. "I can tell."

"His family has been taken," Istvan answered slowly. "It happened last week."

"But Herr Hinkleman was a soloist with the symphony!" Lottie gasped. "Head of the music academy. And his wife and children aren't Jewish. How would the Nazis dare?"

"It doesn't matter who they are," Istvan replied. "The world's gone mad."

"Johann could do nothing?" Lottie asked softly.

Istvan shook his head. "We tried. I am so sorry, my love."

"If the Nazis would murder Herr Hinkleman, then there's no hope for my family." The words tasted bitter in her mouth.

Istvan reached around Lottie's thin shoulders and pulled her close. "No matter what happens, I will be your family now. And never forget how many people we've saved."

The path emptied into a narrow alley. Lottie and Istvan picked their way along the cobblestones as the light waned. On the slope above them, an emaciated cow swayed in the shadows. Rats scurried across the path. At last they came to a small stucco barn. Istvan knocked twice on the heavy wooden door.

"Who's there?" a voice called out.

"It's Johann!" Istvan answered.

"Say the password again?" the voice insisted.

"Johann Schmidt!" Istvan replied.

"Show us!" The door creaked open to reveal the rusted barrel of a rifle. Istvan fished in the pocket of his trousers and pulled out a small pendant on a chain. He flipped it over in his hand. JS was inscribed on the back. Lottie took a matching chain and pendant from the pocket of her jacket. They handed the chains through the crack in the door.

"Come in," the voice commanded.

A group of six or seven young men and women sat on milking stools around a soot-covered stove.

"There's an order for Jews to be rounded up from the Budapest ghetto at the end of the week." A teenage boy wearing a ragged sweater spoke first.

"Have we a plan?" Lottie asked.

The boy shrugged. "We're trying to obtain identity papers, but it's becoming more and more difficult."

"How many do we have?" Istvan sighed.

"Not nearly enough," came the answer.

"I'll give mine," Lottie offered. "I'm safe enough hiding in the hills, and liberation will come soon! It won't be long until—"

"No, you can't," Istvan interrupted her. "The police have been searching, even here in the farthest city gardens. If they find you without papers, you're as good as dead." He gave Lottie a sad smile and squeezed her hand. "We cannot do without you."

"But we must act," Lottie insisted.

"Perhaps we can find more hiding places in the country-side." The young man with the rifle spoke. "I know a wealthy man who is sympathetic and could take two or three families at his vineyard near Lake Balaton."

Several people murmured in agreement.

After the meeting, Lottie and Istvan walked silently up the hillside in the dark. Lottie paused to search the stars beginning to appear above the city. A tear formed and clung to her eyelashes. It had been nearly seven years since she had left her parents and sister in Vienna. "I want to call our first child Rose," she whispered suddenly.

"If it's a girl," Istvan answered, his fingers finding hers. "If it's a boy, I'd like to name him Arpad, after my father."

"Yes, of course." Lottie nodded. "If we have a son, we will remember your father."

She thought back to the days in Vienna, safe in her parents' apartment. It seemed another lifetime entirely. Her little sister, Rose, had liked to hear fanciful stories about princesses and magical creatures. She was especially pleased when the stories had a happy ending: a wedding, or better yet, a miracle.

Reaching deep into her pocket, Lottie felt for the chain and pendant. It had been her cousin Nathan's idea to inscribe a pendant for each member of their resistance group and to use a common German name as their password. Nathan was one of the fortunate ones; he had disappeared after his parents were taken from their village, but Lottie had heard that he was safe in America.

Lottie rubbed the pendant and closed her eyes. In Vienna, she had inscribed the back of a Mogen David with the code, JS. It was of course too dangerous now to possess a Star of David, but Lottie still thought of the pendant as a place of memory; she pressed it against her heart whenever she imagined her family.

Lottie reached up to Istvan's cheek and traced his soft lips with her fingertips. Istvan's family was not Jewish, yet he and his mother and sister had taken her in, sheltered and protected her. Lottie had come to love them like her own family.

"When the war is over, I'm going to buy you a beautiful violin." Istvan's lips curled in a wistful smile. "You will play Mozart for our children."

"Szeretlek." Lottie kissed her darling's mouth. "I love you."

Someday, Lottie thought, someday beyond the madness of this time, there would be music and joy again in the world, and, yes—she smiled—yes, a miracle for her lost little sister—a baby filling the void in her heart with goodness and love.

AUTHOR'S NOTE

The people in this book are my family. That is to say, while all the characters are fictional, many of them are based upon family members whose lives were forever changed by the Holocaust. My grandparents, Herman and Aurelie Lencz, lived in Vienna when the Nazis invaded Austria in 1938. My mother and her brother were able to obtain visas to come to the United States, but my grandparents and most of the rest of my mother's family were unable to escape and perished. My middle name was given in memory of a lovely young cousin named Lotte (or, in English, "Lottie"—short for Charlotte), who was deported and presumed dead. I grew up looking at photos of her bright smile and wondering what her life might have been. Another relative, Magda Szemere, had a brilliant career as a young violin soloist but was killed along with her husband and small son.

My mother arrived in America at age twenty with no money and few friends. She became an American citizen, married, and had five children. Like Nana Rose in the book, Mom rarely talked about the Holocaust; it was too painful. She strove to bring her children up in a world of warmth and love. Just like Nana Rose, Mom had a special saying for nearly every occasion, and these were always full of encouragement. "If at first you don't succeed, try, try again" was one of her favorites. My mother constantly emphasized that the world is a positive, kind place, full of interesting experiences and wonderful human beings. In this way, she surmounted the terrible loss of her family and gave us the gift of love and hope.

Charlie's search for Lottie takes place in 2010. This was when I rediscovered family papers that included Magda Szemere's journal filled with glowing reviews of her performances as a young soloist and realized that with the help of the Internet, I might be able to find out more about my lost relatives. I Googled Magda's name and was stunned to find entries that were not from a Holocaust or genealogy website—rather, there were eBay listings of her gramophone recordings for sale. Magda's and her family's lives had been taken, but her music lived on. To my astonishment, I later discovered that recordings of her music had been preserved in archives in Europe and America.

In 2010, it was still possible that Charlie might find Lottie alive. As time goes on, this ending will of course no longer be feasible. Nevertheless, with the ever-increasing genealogy resources available today, there are limitless opportunities for kids to research and learn about their own family histories.

Most important, however, remain the conversations kids can have with parents and grandparents, sharing family stories and experiences to honor and preserve precious memories. In this way, it is indeed possible to keep the spirit of a lost loved one shining bright.

My relative Charlotte Kulka with her diabolo.